ALLEN COUNTY PUBLIC LIBRARY
3 1833
P9-EDN-995

Texas Drive

Also by Bill Dugan in Large Print:

Brady's Law

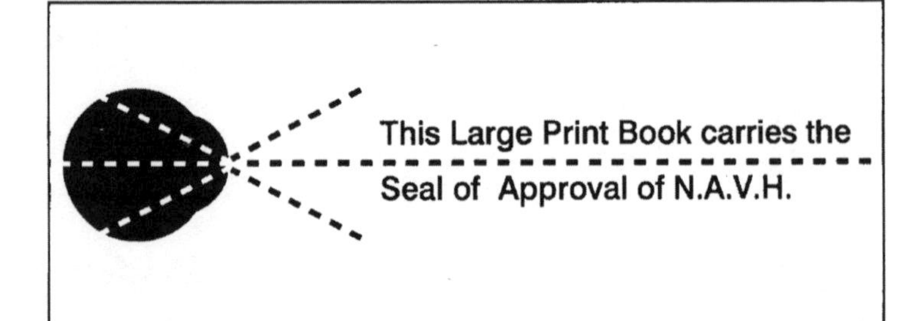

Texas Drive

Bill Dugan

Thorndike Press • Waterville, Maine

This is a work of fiction. Names, characters, places, and incidents are products of the author's imagination or are used fictitiously and are not to be construed as real. Any resemblance to actual events, locales, organizations, or persons, living or dead, is entirely coincidental.

Published in 2005 by arrangement with HarperCollins Publishers.

Thorndike Press® Large Print Western.

The tree indicium is a trademark of Thorndike Press.

The text of this Large Print edition is unabridged. Other aspects of the book may vary from the original edition.

Set in 16 pt. Plantin by Elena Picard.

Printed in the United States on permanent paper.

Library of Congress Cataloging-in-Publication Data

Dugan, Bill.
Texas drive / by Bill Dugan.
p. cm. — (Thorndike Press large print western)
ISBN 0-7862-8095-6 (lg. print : hc : alk. paper)
1. Brothers — Fiction. 2. Ranchers — Fiction. 3. Texas — Fiction. 4. Large type books. I. Title. II. Series: Thorndike Press large print Western series.
PS3563.C3534T49 2005
813′.6—dc22 2005021229

Texas Drive

I

Ted Cotton sat under the only tree for miles around. His mouth tasted like dry grass, and he shook the canteen once before unscrewing the cap. It sounded about a third full, and he checked the sun, then tilted the gritty metal back and let a trickle of water wet his lips and tongue. The water was warm and tasted of metal. Swirling the water around with his tongue, he let it wash some of the dust away, then spat into the sand.

Ted swallowed the second mouthful, shuddering at the unpleasant taste. His brother watched him, sitting against a boulder, trying to keep out of the sun.

"You ought to be glad to have it," Johnny said.

"Hell, sometimes I think I'd rather die of thirst. How come everything in Texas tastes like sand?"

"It ain't Texas, Ted, it's just this part of Texas."

"Big enough part, it might as well be the whole damn state."

"You got to get used to it all over again, that's all."

"I get used to this, I guess hell won't be a problem." Ted took another swig of the bitter water, tried to swallow it without tasting it, and screwed the cap back on the canteen. "I guess I forgot just how bad things were back home."

Johnny ignored him, snatching a dry stalk of grass and scratching at the ground. He seemed lost in thought, and Ted let him alone. He knew his brother well enough to know when he didn't feel like talking.

Getting to his feet, Ted leaned back against the twisted tree, rubbing his back on the rough bark. Shielding his eyes from the sun, he stared into the mouth of Breakneck Canyon. It was almost two o'clock, and the heat rising up off the canyon floor made everything shimmer. The thick, thorny leaves of the tree brushed against his hat, and he stepped away from the gnarled trunk.

"You sure them strays are in there?" Ted asked. He took a couple of steps toward the mouth of the canyon. "There's Rafe," he said, waving his hat.

"About time," Johnny said, groaning as he stood up. "Be nothing but bones we don't get a move on."

"Those steers are too damn tough to die."

"You're probably right, but that meat's tough enough. Folks back east don't want to cut their beef with a hacksaw."

"Folks back east ought to come on out here and get their own damn cows."

"You got a better way to make a living, I'd love to hear about it."

Ted waved his hat again, and this time the approaching rider waved back. In the cloud of dust kicked up behind Rafe, Ted could make out four more riders.

"Seven," he said. "That ought to about do it."

Johnny stretched his arms over his head. "We can't do it with seven, we ought to try another business."

"Maybe we ought to do that anyway."

"Damn it, Teddy, quit bellyaching. Bad enough being out here in the middle of nowhere, without you moaning every damn minute."

Ted clapped the dust from the seat of his pants, but said nothing. He could feel his brother's eyes boring into his back. He wanted to turn around, but knew they'd just have another argument. Johnny was right, anyway. He *did* complain too much. But there wasn't a whole lot else to do.

He felt Johnny's hand on his shoulder. He looked at it, but didn't turn around. Johnny squeezed, and Ted nodded. He understood. They always understood each other. Two years wasn't much of a difference.

Rafe was close enough to shout now, pulling back a little on the reins and letting his horse slow to a fast walk. "You lazy bastards still waiting for me? I thought you'd have all them cows rounded up by now."

Rafe grinned, letting his teeth show without moving his cheeks. It was the strangest smile Ted had ever seen. "You got to earn your pay, too, Rafe," Ted said.

"Pay, is it? I thought this was my hobby. Haven't had two dollars to rub together since before the war."

"Hell, you never had two dollars even then," Johnny said. "Not as long as whiskey was two bits."

Rafe slid from the saddle, coiling the reins tightly in one gloved fist. "You saying I drink a bit, Johnny?" There was that strange grin again.

"A bit . . ."

"Man gets thirsty out here, case you haven't noticed."

Johnny ignored the bait and tugged his own horse toward him with a jerk of the reins. He swung into the saddle, looping one long leg up and over and letting his weight find a comfortable spot in the well-worn leather. Looking at his brother, he said, "You coming, Ted?"

Ted nodded

"Ted's no fool," Rafe said. "He knows what's what."

Johnny waved to the other hands, who were hanging back a little and watching the exchange with amusement. "You boys all ready?"

Dan Harley shook his head. "I guess."

Turning to his brother, Johnny said, "You coming, or not?"

Ted nodded, then climbed onto his mount. "I'm coming."

Johnny wheeled his pony and nudged it toward the mouth of the canyon. Ted brought up the rear, as he always did. It was part reluctance and part habit. Either way, it was where he was most comfortable. Even before the war, Johnny started calling him Drag Rider, after the last man in a trail drive, and Ted had come to like the name, sometimes even going out of his way to provoke his brother by dragging his feet even more than usual.

As they pushed through the broad mouth of Breakneck Canyon, its layers of deep red stone bleached to a dull copper by the brilliant sun, Ted looked up at the rimrock. Huge slabs of red stone seemed to hang on either lip. If he stared at them too long, they wavered, as if the least breeze would send them over and crashing down into the rocky floor far below.

Narrowing his eyes to slits, Ted searched the rim. He felt as if he had missed something, as if there was something he should see up there, but the harder he stared, the more slippery everything became. In the shimmering currents rising off the canyon floor, everything looked as if it were melting, like a candle too close to the fire. Rough edges were smoother, the crags on the canyon walls mortared over with a translucent glaze.

The men ahead of him started to fan out, spreading toward either wall. The canyon slimmed down to a bottleneck, then opened wide. Boulders and thorny brush littered the sandy floor. It was a toss-up which one was harder on the horses and men. The rocks made every step an adventure, but the chaparral and tornillo ripped at their chaps, gouging long furrows in the leather.

Ted knew four men who had lost an eye to the metal hard tornillo thorns, some of them three inches long and sharp as ice picks. Each man picked his own way, knowing the stray cattle could be anywhere, hiding among the boulders or at the end of long channels in the thick brush. The longhorns ate anything, including the thorns, and a spooked steer could send horse and man sprawling into the thicket. Getting out intact was out of the question. Getting out alive was a matter of luck and, to some, a favor from an indifferent God.

Johnny raised the first steer, a rangy bag of hide and bones. The animal raised its head, its nostrils twitching spasmodically. Whatever he was trying to scent, the steer made up his mind in a hurry. With a bellow, it charged out of the rocks, making straight for Johnny's horse. The long horns swung from side to side, dipping like a seesaw, and Johnny narrowly avoided the attack. He spiked himself on some tornillo, one thorn piercing his chaps and snapping off in his calf.

It was going to be a long day.

Four hours later, they had almost a hundred head, all milling in the makeshift corral, raising their heads every time another steer or cow was added. The cows were easier, two for one, because the calves followed wherever the mother went.

Rafe worked harder than the other hands, harder than anyone but Johnny, and Ted watched him wheeling his horse like a man possessed. The little pony looked too small for so big a man. But it was a chopper, used to turning on a dime, and knew the cattle business as well as any man Ted had ever seen. The sun was starting to slip when Rafe finally took off his hat to wipe the sweat from his forehead.

"Reckon you can talk that brother of yours into some chow, Ted?" he said.

"It'll be the first time, if I can," Ted said. He smiled, but Rafe knew he wasn't kidding.

"Shouldn't be so hard on him, son. He only does what your papa taught him to do."

"Papa's dead, Rafe."

Rafe nodded. "I know that."

Ted, feeling he'd made his point, didn't say anything else. He kicked his mount, going easy on the spurs, and went off in search of Johnny. Five minutes later, he found him, tugging a reluctant cow behind him on a short rope. Johnny rode on past, nodding his head. "You lookin' for me?"

"Rafe thinks we ought to knock off for a bit, get something to eat. Sun'll be down soon, anyhow."

"Rafe works for me."

"That means no, I take it?"

"It means what it means."

Ted watched him move away. Johnny's shirt was dark from collar to tail with sweat, a film of sandy dust sticking to the damper places like a thin mud pack. Even the blood-stained right leg of his dungarees wasn't enough to slow him down.

Ted started after his brother, and Tommy Dawson, one of the temporary hands, fell in beside him. "Hot," Tommy said.

Ted nodded. Something, he wasn't sure what, distracted him, and he turned in the saddle. Just off his left shoulder, up among the rocks, something had moved.

He slowed a bit, letting Tommy slide on past him, and stared at the steep face of the canyon wall. Standing in the stirrups, the horse shuffling restlessly under him, he probed the purple stains where shadows had already begun to soak into the rock. He was sure he'd seen something, but the wall was motionless. An eerie quiet filled the canyon.

Ted shook it off, dropping back to the saddle and clucking to the pony. Tommy Dawson was twenty yards ahead now, just a dusty black hat on a pair of broad shoulders. The thornbushes picked up a hint of red from the sun, etching the tan shirt with a lacy network. Then Tommy was gone.

Ted blinked, then he heard the shot. High up, somewhere behind him, it popped, almost like a loud handclap, then echoed off the wall. He spun in the saddle, instinctively searching for the spot where he'd seen the movement. Like before, he saw nothing. Pushing his pony, he charged after Dawson. As he rounded the clump of mesquite bushes, he saw the cowboy on the ground, curled in a ball.

Tommy's horse was long gone. Dawson moaned as Ted jumped from the saddle. Something slammed into his saddle and he turned just as another shot echoed among the rocks.

"Tommy," he shouted, dropping to his knees. Already, he could see the dark red stain high on Dawson's left shoulder. A dark hole just off the shoulder blade seeped blood, and a trickle ran down into the dry sand.

He rolled Dawson over, and the cowboy groaned. One hand lay plastered to the front of his shoulder, and Ted could see the blood oozing between Dawson's fingers, filling the cracks in his skin.

"Sonofabitch," Dawson moaned. His clenched teeth almost obscured the words. Ted tugged a dusty handkerchief from his back pocket and stuffed it between Dawson's fingers and the wound.

"Can you get up, Tommy?"

"Dunno." He tried to sit, wincing as the shoulder moved, and Ted realized the bullet must have broken some bone. "Hold your arm as still as you can." He unknotted Dawson's neckerchief and fashioned a rough sling, looping it under the forearm and reknotting it around Dawson's neck.

"Who done it?" Dawson asked. "You see the bastard?"

Ted shook his head. "Thought I might have seen something up near the rim, but when I looked, there was nothing."

"Nothing, hell," Dawson said, getting to his knees. He tried to stand up, and Ted grabbed Dawson's good arm and draped it over his shoulders.

The first howl came out of nowhere. High-pitched, quavering, it sounded as if someone were being torn apart. Ted almost dropped Dawson.

"The hell was that?" the wounded man asked.

"Comanche . . ."

2

The bloodcurdling howls echoed off the canyon walls, bouncing back at them from a dozen directions. Ted half dragged Dawson toward the foot of the nearest wall. Working sideways, he found a crevice fronted by a pair of boulders and lowered Dawson to the ground.

"You stay here, while I try to get help. Don't move, don't even look out. Whoever nailed you can do it again."

"You think I'm gonna stay here and let some Comanche devil slice my hair off, you better think again."

"Tommy, don't be crazy. I'll get the others and we'll smoke the bastards out."

"According to Johnny, you don't smoke nothin' lately, especially not with no gun."

"Johnny thinks he knows things he doesn't."

Dawson tried to get up, but Ted pushed

him back, none too gently. "Stay down, dammit."

It was quiet again, and Ted cocked an ear toward the rimrock. Off in the distance, he could hear one of the hands yipping at a stray, but that was the only sound. A hot wind riffled sand across the face of the cliff, and Ted looked up. He caught a glimpse of something moving far above him, but then it was gone.

"What is it? What did you see?" Dawson demanded, getting to his feet again. The strain was too much for him, and he leaned back against the rock, groaning. Through clenched teeth, he said, "You sure it's Comanches?"

"How long you lived out here, Tommy?"

"Hell, not long."

"Then don't argue with me. I been here half my life, except for the war. I know what I heard. And Johnny and the others must have heard it, too. Just sit down and wait for me."

Dawson was too weak to argue anymore. He sank down, his shirt scraping the rock and hiking up in back. When he hit bottom, he reached behind him with his good arm and pulled the cloth down between rock and skin.

"Don't stand there gawkin', go get

Johnny and Rafe." He tried to grin, but it didn't work. His lips twisted back, showing his teeth like a mad dog, then he closed the teeth over his lower lip and let out a moan. "Damn, it hurts . . ."

Ted backed away from the crevice, keeping an eye peeled on the rim. He knew the gunshots had come from above and on this side of the canyon. What he didn't know was whether the Indian had any help.

He couldn't see his horse as he backed through the brush, and he was starting to get nervous. The yipping down canyon had died away. The silence had returned. His boots crunched on the dry sand.

Crouching to keep below the thick clumps of mesquite, he swiveled his head back and forth to keep an eye on both sides of the canyon rim. He heard something off to the left, a low muttering, and shifted the Colt nervously in his hand. The sweat on his palms made him feel like he was losing control of the gun. He shifted the Colt to his left hand for a moment to dry his right hand on his shirt.

When he found the horse, he shook his head. The big roan lay on the ground on its side. A pool of blood, already beginning to draw flies, glistened on the sand. The second bullet had pierced the saddle leather, and the horse was finished. It raised its head feebly, nickering once. Ted could see himself in miniature in the big eyes, then the horse lowered its head and lay still.

He jerked a brand-new Winchester carbine from the saddle boot, snatched at his canteen and draped it over his shoulder, then tugged at the saddlebags. He had ammunition for the carbine and his Colt in the bags. The weight of the horse pressed down on one of the bags, and he had to lie on the ground, then brace himself against the animal's flank with both feet and pull to get them free.

It gave way suddenly, and he sprawled backward in the sand. As he lay there, he spotted a figure high on the rim, beginning to climb down not thirty yards from where Dawson lay hidden.

Cursing under his breath, he got to his knees, levered a shell into the carbine's chamber, and drew a bead. There was no question it was a Comanche. He could see the distinctive markings clearly as the Indian turned his head to one side, hugging the stone on his way down the wall. Like a brightly colored fly.

He hesitated, telling himself he would wait for a better shot. The Comanche straddled an outcropping, seeming to balance for a moment, then dropped two or three feet, scrabbling at the wall with his feet. Watching the Indian over his gunsight, Ted felt a strange detachment, as if the descending brave had nothing to do with him.

Moving to one side, to get a better look, he resighted. It was a clear shot, dead on, and he started to squeeze the trigger. He felt his finger curl, then stop. He got up and started to run toward the wall. Another Comanche, then a third and a fourth, appeared on the canyon rim.

All three started shooting at him. He heard the bullets sing past him, snapping twigs and brittle leaves. They slammed into the sand and whined off the rocks. The climbing Indian dropped another three feet, as if he were not part of what was happening above and below him.

Ted dove behind a boulder and fired once at the Indians on the rim. The bullet chipped hunks of red stone free, and they cascaded down the wall, just to the Comanche's right.

As Ted charged toward the base of the cliff, the Indian on the wall spotted him. Ted started to move faster, but the Indian was faster still.

The Comanche pushed away from the wall and dropped out of sight, still forty feet above the canyon floor. Ted was close enough to hear the Comanche grunt when he hit, and picked up speed. Behind him, he heard hoofbeats, but there was no time to look. Gunshots cracked through the thick air, and splinters of rock began to rain down, skittering across the rocky face of the cliff like stone spiders.

Ted could no longer see the Indians above him, but they were returning fire at the charging riders behind him. The Comanche from the wall reappeared, limping now, and Ted broke toward the left, trying to head him off before he found Tommy. The brave stopped long enough to fire once, then dodged behind a rock.

Hitting the ground, he lay there panting for a moment, trying to catch his breath. He couldn't see the Comanche, and with the ruckus behind him, there was no chance of hearing him, either. He got to his feet and raised the carbine, but there was nothing to shoot at.

He could see the boulders where Dawson lay now, but there was no sign of the Indian. The firing above him had stopped, but a howl echoed through the canyon, and he turned to see more than a dozen Comanches on the far rim. They opened up all at once. He dove to the ground again, but the Indians weren't shooting at him. The hoofbeats had stopped, and Ted knew Johnny and the other hands had dismounted. They started shooting at the Indians behind them, and Ted turned his back. He saw the Comanche now, poised on a boulder.

Ted snapped a shot from the Winchester, but it missed badly, and the Indian jumped to another rock. He teetered a moment, and Ted could see the blood streaming from a bad gash on the Comanche's thigh.

He fired twice more, the second time just as the Indian dropped out of sight. The bullet slammed into the wall, waist high where the Indian had been. Ted scrambled through the heavy brush. A thorn ripped his right sleeve from the elbow to the cuff as he charged past. He closed on the crevice. The Comanche stood there, straddling Dawson, who held one hand up in front of his face.

Ted took a step forward, then froze. The Indian sensed him and turned. For a moment, he stood still, his painted face hovering over his shoulder, as if waiting to see what Ted would do. Footsteps sounded behind him, and he turned to see Johnny charging toward him.

"Shoot him, dammit, what are you waiting for?"

The Indian, released by the shout, raised his right hand. Ted could see the knife as it caught the setting sun, glittering like gold for a split second. He fired as the arm started down. Johnny brushed past him, emptying his revolver at the crouching Comanche.

The knife slid from his fingers and clattered on the stone. Dawson cried out as Johnny charged into the crevice, with Ted on his heels.

"Bastard," Johnny shouted, grabbing the Indian by the shoulders and hurling him backward. His head slammed into a rock and Johnny dove on him. He jerked the brave's head up and slammed it again into the rock, then again, and a third time.

"Stop it, Johnny! He's dead, stop it . . ."

Ted grabbed at his brother and tried to tear him away, but Johnny turned and swung at him. He snatched at the knife and plunged it into the Comanche's throat, ripping the blade sideways, then plunging it in again.

Ted wrestled him away from the dead Comanche, but Johnny flung him aside.

Panting, his right hand covered with blood, he stared at his brother.

"You damned coward. He could have killed Tommy. Why didn't you shoot him?"

"I did, dammit. I did shoot him."

"What the hell took you so long?" Johnny pushed past him and headed back across the canyon floor. He didn't look back. Dawson lay there moaning. He stared at Ted with confusion and disappointment in his eyes. Then he shook his head and turned away.

Ted wanted to say something, but he couldn't find the words. He turned to follow Johnny back into the chaparral. With the carbine dangling from one hand, he ran straight up. The Comanches on the rim spotted him and started firing. He ignored the slugs whistling past him, kicking up spouts of sand on either side.

Just ahead, he could hear the hands firing sporadically at the rim. By the time he reached the other hands, the Comanches on the rim had started to break off the attack. Once the surprise failed, they weren't interested. Johnny and Rafe and the others chewed at the rimrock until their guns were empty.

Johnny turned as Ted finished reloading his own weapon. "What the hell are you doing here? Why didn't you stay with Dawson?"

"I thought I was needed here."

"Yeah, well . . . It's over." Johnny spat into the dry ground, grinding the damp spot under the toe of one boot. "No thanks to you, neither."

"Let him alone, Johnny," Rafe said.

Johnny glared at the older man. "Rafe, butt out. This is family business. Understand? This is between me and Ted."

"I only meant you should . . ."

Johnny interrupted him. "I don't give a damn what you meant, Rafe. I know what you meant, but I don't give a damn."

Rafe shrugged his shoulders. "Have it your way, son."

Without another word to his brother, Johnny shouted to the hands, strung out in a crooked line among the thickets. "Back to work, you lazy bastards. We got some beeves to round up."

Rafe watched him as he stalked away, then turned to Ted. "That boy's heading for trouble, Teddy. You keep an eye on him, will you?"

Ted nodded. "If he lets me."

"Don't pay that no mind. He didn't mean nothing by it."

"The hell he didn't, Rafe."

3

Ted Cotton sat on the front porch, hacking at a cottonwood branch as thick as his wrist. The sun was sinking as Johnny pushed through the rusty screen door out onto the porch.

He looked at his brother for a long time without saying anything. Ted continued to slice curls off the cottonwood without acknowledging his brother. In the evening quiet, the only sound was the whisper of the steel through the soft wood and softer bark. Each curl fell into his lap as he rocked, occasionally pushing himself with one leg braced against the porch railing.

Johnny dropped to the top step and leaned against the column of bleached wood holding up the roof. He tugged one heel under him and stretched the other leg across the top of the steps. He lit a cigarette, then tossed the match away with a snap of his wrist. Ted glanced at him, and at the tight stream of exasperated smoke swirling away on the breeze.

"You ain't gonna say anything at all, are you?" Johnny asked.

Ted didn't answer right away.

"Because if you ain't, then maybe you ought to just listen. Sit there and hack at that damn wood and listen."

"I'm listening."

"I don't want to be here no more."

"This spread?"

"Texas."

"I thought you liked it here."

"I thought you was my brother."

"I am."

"Don't seem like it. Don't seem to me like any brother of mine, any son of my daddy for that matter, would've done what you done yesterday."

"Which was . . . ?"

"Stand there and watch a goddamned Comanche come within a cunt hair of slitting your best friend's throat. That ain't no brother of mine done that, I swear."

"I killed the man, didn't I?"

"What? Oh, hell yes, you killed him. Just about barely, though. I didn't come along, maybe you wouldn't have done it even then, which as it was was almost too damn late for Tommy Dawson."

"That what he said?"

"No, that ain't what he said. Tommy ain't said nothing at all about it. That don't mean he ain't thinking about it though, I guarantee."

Ted whittled for a while before answering. "Where you going to go?"

"I get another couple hundred cows, I believe I might take 'em on up to Kansas, see can I find someplace I like better'n here."

"You want me to go with you?"

"What do you think?"

"I don't know. Sounds to me like you wish I wasn't your kin. That bein' so, maybe you'd like it just fine if I was to stay here."

Johnny sucked on the cigarette, looked at it in disgust, and tossed it into the yard. "Don't go stupid on me, Teddy. You're my brother. Nothing can change that. I wouldn't mind if something was to change you, but I can't help that. Hell, I don't know, maybe you can't, neither."

"What's that supposed to mean?"

"It means what it means. It also means I got to be sure you can pull your own weight, you come along with me. It means I got to be able to tell Tommy and Rafe they don't have to worry if you're along and we run into some goddamned redskins."

"I'll think about it."

"You do that . . ." Johnny got up and walked off the porch. Ted watched him stalk toward the barn, digging his heels in harder than necessary, as if he were trying to scrape something off his boots.

He disappeared into the rickety barn, then reappeared with a saddle over his shoulder. Ted watched as the older man saddled his pinto pony, then swung into the stirrups with a practiced ease.

He whittled a little faster until Johnny was gone out of sight, then stuck the knife into the rail and stood up. The shavings spilled onto the weatherbeaten porch floorboards and crinkled under his feet as he stepped to the screen door. Inside, he went to his room and closed the door. Red light from the west spilled into the room as he sat on his lumpy mattress. It stained his hands, and he stared at the bloody-looking fingers, curling them this way and that, interlacing them, then tugging them apart again.

When the sun finally slipped below the horizon, and the red light was gone, he reached for his gunbelt, strapped it on, and left the house. He saddled his own pony, mounted up, and walked the horse past the bunkhouse.

Rafe MacCallister was sitting outside. Ted could see the ember of a cigarette end in the shadows.

"Late to be goin' for a ride, ain't it, son?"

"Never too late for anything, Rafe."

"Wish that was so, Ted, wish that was so."

"See you later, Rafe."

"Where you going?"

"I need to think a little bit."

"You be careful, boy. Them Comanches will likely be looking to get even. They don't like to lose."

"You tell Johnny that just now?"

"Course I did. Why wouldn't I?"

Ted nodded, then kicked his pony into a slow trot. He waved his hat, knowing that Rafe probably couldn't see him, but wanting to acknowledge the old man anyway. And he knew very well where he was going. There was little doubt in his mind that Rafe also knew. But some things were unnecessary to say while others were better left unsaid. In this case, it was a little of both, unnecessary to tell Rafe, and just as well unsaid as far as his brother was concerned.

Riding through the dark and peaceful countryside, he concentrated on his pony's hoofbeats, the way a man waiting for something will concentrate on a clock. It sometimes seemed he knew exactly how many strides of his pony it would take to get from one place to another. That was a consequence, he knew, of his rather limited inclination to move any great distance from the house, except when work required it. And when he did go, there were few places he was willing to go.

Unlike Johnny and the other hands, he avoided San Pedro. He was not a great drinker, and there were only two reasons to visit the town. Both involved whiskey. One of them also involved women who were less than scrupulous about the company they kept, and the degree of intimacy with which they kept it. For that matter, they seemed unconcerned about the frequency, as well.

Ted knew that he had been changed by what happened at Shiloh. He still had nightmares. They squeezed him in the dark like a fistful of giant fingers crushing his chest. He would wake up gasping for air, soaked in sweat and thrashing around in his bed like a man on fire. And without exception, the nightmares stopped just short of his own death. He would find himself staring into the muzzle of a Yankee musket. He could see the musket ball, just beginning to emerge from the barrel of the gun. Its surface was rough, pitted like the moon through his father's old telescope.

He'd had that one a hundred times, maybe a thousand. But they were all variations on the same theme. The smell was what lingered. He would wake up with the smell of blood and voided bowels so thick in the air it felt as if he were trying to swim across a glue pot. Everything tugged at him. His movements were sluggish to the point of futility. Great strings of red mucilage pulled at his arms as he tried to raise them above the surface, crawling for his life through a fluid too thick to let him drown, but too strong to let him go. And those first few minutes never failed to take a lifetime.

His breathing would be labored for an hour. He was forced to lay there in the dark, unwilling, even unable, to close his eyes. What he saw in the dark was too plain, and too horrible, to stand.

But he blamed himself. He thought it must be some weakness in him, some hidden flaw. Johnny had been there with him, but he seemed, if anything, tougher since Shiloh, not softer. What had begun to eat at him like invisible rust had tempered Johnny. What was toughness in his brother had become, according to some, including Rafe, a mean streak. Maybe Johnny had handled it the right way. And that uncertainty made his own reaction even harder to bear.

Ted eased his horse back into a walk, letting the pony wander without direction. As they approached the San Pedro Creek, the animal stopped to pull at some foot-high grass, munching contentedly a few moments after each mouthful before moving on a few yards to the next clump of grass. At this rate, he knew, it would take him hours to get where he was going. But that was a blessing. At least he wouldn't have to face the horrors of sleep.

After two hours, the moon rose above the horizon, its pale silver light spilling through the scattered trees and glistening on the water. At places where rocks broke the surface of the slow-moving stream, the turbulence burbled and reflected the light in patches of cold, white fire. He was only dimly aware of them, like landmarks too familiar to be noticed.

When the first glimpse of light bobbed into view across the creek, he tugged his pony away from its careless grazing and poked it with his knees. The pony shook him off once, then broke into a trot again. He sawed on the reins, urging the animal into the water and across the creek. He could feel the water rise just above his boots. Usually he would hoist his feet up above the water, but this time he was too preoccupied to care. He felt the creek pour into his boots, and when the pony finally climbed out on the opposite bank, he could hear the water sloshing in them. It sounded like maracas full of damp seeds, squishing dully as his legs rose and fell with the rhythm of the pony's gait.

The horse seemed to sense his anxiety and pulled against the reins, trying to take its head. The light grew a little brighter, then stayed steady as the house in which it sat grew slowly more substantial. Ted had no idea of the time, but he gave no thought to turning back. He couldn't, not now, not tonight. He needed to talk to someone who would understand, someone with whom he could share the conflicting emotions churning inside him.

He could see the house clearly now and kicked the horse a little to urge it forward. He skidded to a halt in front of a sun-bleached hitching post and flicked the reins. They wound around the post on their own, and he fashioned a quick half hitch to keep them secure, then mounted the stairs, trying to muffle the sound of his feet on the wooden steps.

The screen door swung open as he climbed the last step. He could see her outlined against the dull glow of the lamp from the living room behind her. She held one hand to her mouth, as if she had been chewing on her knuckles.

"Sorry it's so late, Ellie."

"Thank God you're alright, Ted. I was so worried. Everybody was talking about it. I didn't know what to think."

"I still don't. Is your father awake?"

"No, Daddy's gone to bed. I'll wake him if you want."

"No, that's alright."

She moved to a swing suspended from the porch roof beams. Patting the seat beside her, she said, "Sit here."

"No, I don't think I can sit still. I'll just sit on the railing." He hoisted himself up and balanced precariously on the rail, careful to avoid splinters from the dry, split oak of the banister.

He watched her in the near dark as she glided back and forth. She seemed to disappear in the shadows for a moment, then float toward him. Just when it seemed she was close enough to reach out and touch, she started back, to disappear again a few seconds later.

"Johnny's leaving," he said.

"What? To go where? How can he?"

"Says he wants to take a herd up north. Says he can't stand Texas anymore."

"You going with him?" she asked. He could tell by the edge in her voice what she wanted to hear.

"I don't think he wants me to."

"What do you want? That's more important."

"No, it isn't. Nothing's more important than family. But if I want to go, and he doesn't want me along, seems like I have no right to go."

"He's your brother."

"I know that. But it doesn't change anything."

"But . . ."

"I don't think I want to talk about it, Ellie. Not now. Not yet. If it's all the same to you, I'd like to be here without talking."

"I'll make some coffee. I think it's going to be a long night."

4

The herd had swollen to nearly three thousand head, most of them rawhide tough and stringy. Johnny was talking about getting some English white faces when he got north, but that took money, and the herd was the family fortune. Night riding, Ted had a lot of time to think. He still hadn't told Johnny whether he would go, and Johnny hadn't asked. For that, Ted didn't know whether to be grateful or resentful.

Rafe kept watching him, as if he expected some sort of transformation. But Ted wasn't changing. Not that he knew of, anyway. He did his job and kept away from the other hands, sleeping during the day while they tried to round up a few hundred more. Johnny had taken a half-dozen men over the border into Mexico, but he came back with almost as many exhausted horses as he did cows. He wouldn't talk about it, but it appeared they had narrowly missed getting bushwhacked by a bunch of Mexicans and had to leave nearly three hundred cows behind.

The moon was almost full now, and the cattle huddled together, lowing quietly. As they shuffled their feet, their backs, silvered by the moon, looked almost like a huge lake. They were leaving in two days, and Ted knew he had to decide by the following night.

He didn't want to go, but he wasn't sure why. He knew he didn't want to leave Ellie, and her father would never let her tag along. He thought about asking her to marry him, but he was too young and probably too scared. So his choice boiled down to staying with her or riding out of her life, because Johnny had no intentions of coming back. Kansas was a long way, and Ted knew he'd never come back alone, even if he wanted to.

He was on his third circuit of the herd when he saw something move on the far edge. Ted stood in the stirrups to get a better look, but whatever it was had stopped. He prodded his pony and nudged it into the herd. The cows shuffled aside as the pony waded through. He noticed some stirring at the far edge, as if something had spooked the cattle.

Halfway across, he saw it again and this time there was no mistake. A man on foot was moving along the outer edge of the herd. It looked as if he didn't know he'd been spotted. Ted drew his Colt, but couldn't fire without starting a stampede. He was almost across when he got another look at the intruder.

A Comanche, in full regalia, slipped along the edge of the herd. Ted watched him, but couldn't figure out what the Indian was trying to do. But he also knew that there would be more of them, out there in the dark. The cattle had gotten very restless, nudging one another and raising their heads to sniff the wind. They started to move a bit now, milling in a circle.

A spurt of flame lit up the Indian for a moment, then died down. The Indian dropped out of sight, but the dim orange glow persisted. He could smell smoke now and kicked his horse harder. A second and third spurt of flame blossomed, both of them closer to the front edge of the herd, near the chuck wagon.

The Comanches were trying to stampede the herd. The dry, brittle grass of late summer, almost explosively flammable with the long absence of rain, was already beginning to burn. The flames licked along the outer edge of the herd as Ted broke through, the cattle sensed the flames and backed away, kicking at the earth in their fear. If they got moving, there would be no stopping them.

Ted jumped from his horse and ripped his saddle loose. Snaring the blanket, he raced toward the first fire and started to swat the flames. Every stroke of the blanket sent coils of flaming embers up into the air where they winked out and drifted off like black snow.

He beat the first fire to ashes, but four more were burning, and the nearest steers were pushing nervously at the herd. The sharp tang of burnt grass filled the air as Ted raced to the second fire. A shot cracked in the dark, and a bullet whined past his hip and slammed into a calf. Ted turned to see the animal stagger once, then fall to its knees. The shot did what the fire was meant to, and the cows started to bellow.

Already, Ted could hear the distant thunder of hooves as the far side of the herd started to run, the steers on the edge pressured by the cattle behind them. Ted flailed at the second fire, ignoring the fact that it was already too late to stop the stampede.

He heard shouts in the distant darkness, then yips as two or three of the hands mounted up and tried to head off the cattle before they got up a full head of steam. Ted moved to the third fire and raised the blanket again. He had started down when he caught something in the corner of his eye. He turned as he realized what it was. The Comanche, a knife in his left hand, hurtled toward him, and Ted swung the blanket down. He knew it wouldn't stop the knife, but the Indian was already too close for him to step aside.

Ted fell backward, twisting the thick wool as he rolled to one side. He'd snared the Indian and twisted again as he tried to get up. The Comanche's hand flailed at him, the blade narrowly missing him as he tripped again. Ted kicked out with his left leg and landed a glancing blow on the Comanche's ribs. The Indian grunted with the impact and fell to one knee. Ted grabbed for the Colt on his hip and brought it up as the Indian jerked his arm free of the snare.

He fired point-blank, and the Comanche jerked upright for a second, then toppled over on his side. In the moonlight, the blood seeping from the Indian's chest looked like liquid coal. Ted scrambled to his feet and bent over him. The Indian looked up, his lips curled back in hatred. In the orange light of the lingering flames he looked almost demonic.

Ted cocked his Colt and aimed it. The Comanche tried to get to his feet, but he didn't have the strength. Propped on one hip, he lay there panting. Ted turned away, lowering the hammer and holstering the gun. The brave was no threat.

Snatching at the blanket, he raced to the next fire and flailed at the flames until they were reduced to glowing straws. The light rose and fell as the wind moaned past, then they died out altogether. In the distance, he could hear the hands rounding the herd and driving it to let the cattle run off their terror.

Scattered gunshots cracked over the thunder of the hooves. He saw another Comanche, this one on horseback, race toward him. Hitting the ground, he grabbed the Colt and snapped off a shot. The Indian charged past, tossing a lance, but didn't stop. The lance grazed Ted, piercing his shirt and pinning him to the ground. He ripped the cloth away, wiped the blood on his shirt, and got to his knees.

He turned, waiting for the Indian to charge back, but the sound of the horse receded in the night. When it was gone, he got to his feet, holding his side. He could feel the trickle of blood between his fingers, hot and sticky. He could smell it and wanted to gag.

Ted walked toward the Comanche, who was lying on his back now. Behind him, he heard hoofbeats and reached for his gun. Johnny skidded to a halt. He dismounted and raced toward his brother.

"What the hell happened? Where were you?"

"What are you talking about?"

"You know damn well. How did this happen? Why the hell were you night riding, to watch the goddamned moon?"

Johnny spotted the Comanche and brushed past. He prodded the Indian in the ribs with the toe of one boot. The brave moaned. His eyes opened and he stared up at Johnny.

"Christ almighty, he ain't even dead! Can't you do nothing right?"

"He was no . . ."

Johnny drew his gun and cocked the hammer. Ted grabbed his arm, but Johnny shook him off.

"Don't . . ." Ted shouted, but Johnny ignored him. He fired once, then again, hitting the Indian in the head and the heart. Johnny turned, shaking his head.

"You yellow bastard . . ." He brushed past Ted, glanced at the wound in his side, but said nothing. Johnny grabbed the reins and swung up into the saddle. "We're leaving first light. No thanks to you, we have enough beeves to head north. I don't imagine you'll be comin'."

Johnny wheeled his horse and galloped away. Ted stood there watching horse and rider disappear. When his brother was out of sight, he glanced at the dead Comanche once, then walked back to his horse. It hurt to mount up but he ignored the pain and spurred the pony once, just hard enough to get him moving.

The sound of the herd off in the distance was growing more subdued, even as he approached. He moved past the mess wagon, but didn't stop. He skirted the edge of the herd, now just milling in a broad circle. He spotted a hand, but couldn't tell it was Rafe until he got closer.

Rafe looked at him long and hard, but didn't say anything until their mounts were almost nose to nose.

"You see Johnny?" he asked.

Ted nodded.

Rafe saw the blood and started to ask a question, then changed his mind. "I got work, Teddy. See you in the morning."

"Where's Johnny now?"

"Riding point."

"Thanks."

"I'd give him some time, I was you. He was madder'n hell."

Ted ignored the advice. He pushed his pony around the edge of the herd and prodded it into a gallop. He passed two hands on the way, but they didn't acknowledge him. When he reached the head of the herd, he spotted Johnny almost immediately.

He closed on his brother, nudging his horse alongside, squeezing in between Johnny and Ralph Dalton. Dalton spat once, then shook his head as he moved away.

"Johnny . . ."

His brother didn't answer.

"Dammit, Johnny, talk to me."

"Must be hearing things," Johnny mumbled. "Swear I heard something." He turned and looked through Ted as if he were a pane of glass. "Nope. Don't see nothing."

Ted grabbed Johnny's arm and jerked it. The sleeve of Johnny's shirt started to groan, but it held and Johnny clapped a hand over Ted's wrist. This time he spoke directly to him.

"You let go or I'll break your god-damned arm, you hear?"

Ted swung, but missed. Johnny leapt from the saddle, swatting the pony on the rump to chase it away. "Come on, you damned yellow-belly. Come on!"

Ted kicked his pony and threw himself on Johnny as the horse moved past. They both went sprawling in the dust, and Johnny, who was the larger of the two, grabbed Ted around the head and got to his knees.

"Let go," Ted shouted, his voice almost strangled in his throat by the pressure of his brother's arm. He broke free and landed a vicious jab to Johnny's ribs. Doubled over by the punch, Johnny charged straight on, his head smashing into Ted's bleeding rib cage.

Johnny straightened him up and swung twice, connecting both times. Ted fell to the ground and Johnny stood over him, a fist cocked, and panting. "Too late for heroics, Teddy. You had your chance. Trouble is, you just don't know what side you're on. Now get up and get out of my sight."

Ted tried to rise, but his side hurt too much. A searing pain flared along his ribs, and it stabbed at him with every breath. Johnny turned and walked away. When he reached his horse, he mounted without looking back.

"Wait," Ted called, "come back."

But Johnny ignored him. Rafe reined in as Ted was getting to his knees. "You want me to go after him?"

Ted shook his head. "What's the use?"

"None that I can see. Not right now . . ."

"Thanks anyway."

"He'll cool down some, pretty soon."

"Yeah."

But Ted knew he wouldn't. Not for a long time, if ever.

5

Ted Cotton sat on the ridge, watching the herd move out. The valley below him was filled with the sound of bellowing cattle. Their hooves kicked up great clouds of dust. The clouds swirled in a hot wind, obscuring parts of the herd and wrapping the drovers in a thick blanket of light brown. Here and there, one of the hands would pop into view for a few seconds, his face covered with a kerchief to keep out the choking dust. Hats, shirts, and pants had turned a uniform beige.

Ted wanted to see Johnny one more time. But the dust and the wind conspired to deprive him. Tempted to charge down into the valley, he struggled and overcame it, but not without cost. He hated to see Johnny go like this. But his brother was pigheaded. And something ate at him from the inside. Johnny wouldn't talk about it, but he wasn't much for talking anyway. Shrugging his shoulders, Ted resigned himself to the possibility he might never see Johnny again.

The herd, like a heaving river of sinew, poured through the valley, funneled through its narrow mouth, and gradually disappeared. When it was out of sight, he could still hear it. The shouts of the drovers were no longer audible, but the thunder of twelve thousand hooves shook the air around him. He could feel the ground rumbling even through his horse's legs and up through his own. It felt as if the earth were shifting beneath him the least little bit, trying to make up its mind which way to go. Slowly the sound and trembling died away, leaving only the dust cloud, a pale brown stain on an otherwise unblemished blue sky.

Then the cloud, too, was gone.

Ted still sat on his horse, wondering what would become of him. He wondered whether he should have toughed it out, forced himself on Johnny. It was his right. They were brothers, after all. But Johnny didn't want him along. Maybe it was even worse than that. Maybe Johnny was glad to be leaving him behind, glad at the prospect of never seeing him again.

And maybe Johnny was right. Maybe there *was* something wrong with him. Maybe . . . but the list was endless. There was nothing he could do about it anyway. Johnny was gone, taking with him the only living connection to a past already so distant it might have belonged to someone else.

He thought about going to see Ellie. But there was nothing she could say that would change things. What had happened had happened. The only thing he didn't know was why.

Johnny didn't say much that morning. All through the afternoon, he rode apart from the herd, keeping up, just not keeping close. His mind was blank and he felt numb. For long stretches, he felt as if he were watching himself from somewhere above. He could look down, even saw the top of his hat, a dusty speck on a dusty man riding a dusty horse. He knew what he was watching, but he didn't recognize himself.

There were too damn many questions, and he had damn few answers. It was better not to try to connect the few and the many. That would leave questions he could have no hope of answering at all. It was the right thing to do. He kept telling himself that over and over. Ted would only get himself killed. Or he might get someone else killed. Not intentionally, of course, but still . . .

Rafe tried to cheer him up, but the old man knew what was eating him, and it kept getting in the way. This was something you couldn't pretend about. It was sitting there between them, a huge rock of uncertainty, and there was no way either man could budge it. Finally, Rafe shrugged and rode back to the herd. Maybe with time, Johnny thought, he could talk about it. And when he was ready, Rafe would be there. Both of them knew that, and it made it easier.

But not much.

By noon, the sun had hammered at them for so long, Johnny was already wondering whether he'd made a mistake. He looked up at the sun, tilting his hat back to take the full force of its glare. Through closed eyes, he saw a pink haze and white light like the tip of a glowing poker. It stabbed at him, but he refused to turn away. That wasn't the kind of man he was.

Without thinking about it, he understood that changing his mind about anything was not permitted. He didn't know how to change his mind. It was something you made up, and then you lived with it, come hell or high water. And the late summer sun promised him plenty of the former.

It would be months before he would sleep on the same spot of ground twice in a row. And that thought didn't faze him. It didn't cheer him, either. It was the choice he had made. And maybe, if he kept his scalp and his herd, he could send for Ted, and they could talk it through.

If Ted would come.

Johnny kicked his pony and spurted far out ahead of the herd. This was all new to him, and he wasn't sure how he ought to go about it. It was one thing to round up a small herd and drive it to New Orleans, the way he had once or twice before the war. But New Orleans wasn't paying enough to make it worth the trip anymore. The real market was back east, maybe St. Louis, maybe Chicago, definitely New York and Boston. But he had to get the cattle to a railhead. That the nearest one was fifteen hundred miles away didn't help much.

If you're going to drive a herd over a thousand miles, he thought, why not two thousand? Or three? The logistics were the same, it just took more time. As he sat on a ridge a mile and a half ahead of the herd, he turned in the saddle and watched the beeves flow up and over the last rise, oozing like mud. The cattle seemed almost playful, spurting ahead here and there, the herd changing shape like a ball of wax in the sun.

But they were more than beeves. They were his past and his future. It was all he had on earth, that and a few hundred dollars for supplies. To feed his hands, buy ammunition, take care of whatever surprises might sneak up on them until they got where they were going, wherever the hell that was.

Rafe was unsure, arguing they should head west to New Mexico, where they knew the army was buying beef. But Johnny wouldn't hear of it. He trusted Rafe, loved him even. The old man was the closest thing he had to a father. But a man had to make his own decisions. That's what being a man was all about. And that's what got Teddy all twisted up, trying to listen to that damn Ellie and her Quaker nonsense.

This was no place to be peaceful. The war had taught him that, and he'd seen nothing since it ended to change his mind. Ellie had softened Teddy, sapped his strength with all her nonsense about loving Indians as well as white men. You couldn't do that. You couldn't even think of them as human, if they were at all, because they'd cut your heart out and eat it raw if you gave them the chance.

Ellie had almost gotten Tommy Dawson killed. Johnny was convinced of that. If she hadn't filled Ted's head with such plain horseshit, he wouldn't have blinked an eye before killing that Comanche. But she had, and he did. And that was all there was to it.

But the country would toughen Ted up again. Long after it chewed Ellie and her kind up and spat out the bones, Ted would still be there, because he knew how tough it was. He would see how foolish Ellie's thinking was. If she lasted, if she lived, the country would change her, too. It would make her more like Teddy used to be, ought to be. If she didn't, Teddy would be free and clear. Either way, he'd have his brother back.

If he lived long enough.

As the herd closed in on him, sweeping down the broad slope, painting the sky above it a dull brown, he wished to hell things could have been different. It would be good to know that Teddy was bringing up the rear, the way he always had, ever since they were kids. That's when they first started calling him Drag Rider. It had stuck, and Teddy had always been happy with it. But not now. Teddy didn't listen to him anymore. Teddy wanted to go his own way, live by his own rules. Maybe that's what hurt the most, not having the final say anymore.

He watched the herd draw closer, and knew that was only part of it. He still couldn't shake the feeling that something had gutted his brother, stripped off something he used to have. And that it could get them both killed.

Better him than me, Johnny thought, as he wheeled his pony and started down to the floor of the next valley. And he hated himself for thinking that.

"It's your own damn fault, little brother," he whispered. "Not mine."

And Johnny almost believed it.

The day was empty. Texas stretched as far as Ted could see. And as far as he could see, it was empty. Hot and dry, but featureless, like hell without imagination. Sitting on the porch, he turned his attention to the rest of his life. From here, it looked as empty as Texas itself. Stretching out far enough that he couldn't see the end, but end it would. In some ways it already had.

The bottle of whiskey was two-thirds gone, and it hadn't made him feel any better. Maybe the last third would make a difference. At least he wasn't afraid to find out.

He tilted the bottle up and took a long pull of the foul-tasting stuff. His taste ran more to beer, and little of that. He'd tried whiskey during the war, in Tennessee. It was supposed to be the best in the world, except for something from Scotland. But he hadn't liked it then and three years had done precious little to change his mind. The stuff still tasted like it was trying to burn its way out, scorching him from his tongue all the way down.

He shrugged and took another pull. "What the hell's the difference?" He looked around, as if someone else had spoken.

But the porch was empty, and so was the earth, as far as he could see. He had only felt this lonely once in his life, at Shiloh, staring right up the muzzle of a Yankee rifle. The black hole looked big enough to swallow him, and the black eyes behind it looked deeper and darker still. Only a misfire had saved him, and for a moment he had been sorry, wishing to hell it was all over. He wanted the noise to stop, the terrible thunder of the guns, the screaming of wounded men, the sighing of the wind in those rare moments when no one fired and no one spoke. But most of all, he wanted the stink to go away. The stench of blood, the smell of piss, and the almost-sweet fragrance of gunsmoke, hanging like a shroud over them all, Rebel and Federal alike.

But it hadn't gone away. None of it had. The sounds were still rattling around inside his skull, and the stench clung to his skin. He couldn't rub, wash, or scrape it away, and now he no longer tried. It would stay with him until he drew his last breath. He still wondered why no one else seemed to notice it. Even Ellie, who got closer to him than anyone else, didn't notice. Or if she did, she chose not to mention it.

But it was there.

He emptied the bottle and tossed it into the yard. It clattered across the ground but didn't break. That made him angry. He wanted it to break, and when it didn't, he fished his Colt out of its holster and fired, but he missed by several feet. He fired again and came no closer.

When the gun was as empty as the bottle, it still lay there, mocking him. He wanted to break it in the worst way, but couldn't. He tried to get up, but he was too drunk and fell back in the chair, fighting to keep from throwing up.

As the sun started to go down, the bottle changed colors, the white flash of the glass changing to orange, then to red. Finally, in one last wink of purple, it was gone. No longer taunted by the glass, he closed his eyes and slept.

6

Johnny reined in on the hilltop. Rafe skidded to a halt alongside of him.

"There it is, Rafe, the Arkansas River. We get wet one more time, and we're in Kansas."

"Seems like nothing, Johnny, don't it? I mean hell, what's one more river? All them politicians drawing lines back in Washington. Cows don't pay any attention to lines. Maybe they got more sense than we do."

"I guess they do, Rafe. Still, we come all this way, we might as well celebrate, don't you think?"

"I don't have the strength to celebrate, Johnny. I'm an old man."

"You got more than I do. More than the boys, too."

"Nope, I don't. But it sure is pretty in a funny way, all them rolling hills. Some kind of paradise, looks like. Almost, anyhow."

"I was thinking, Rafe. Maybe we shouldn't stop here."

"You better be kidding, Johnny. The boys are a whisker from half dead. You want to push them farther, they won't like it. You'll lose half of them, and them that stay won't be up to much."

"I look at the herd, Rafe, and you know what I see? I see money. I see the future. If we can push on, maybe to Wyoming, someplace like that, we can build a spread. Sell off enough of the beeves to get a stake, keep the rest and build on 'em."

"You can't push them cows no more, either, Johnny. They're already worn to the knees. Bags of bones, most of 'em. You make them walk to Wyoming, they'll be saddlebags on bloody stumps before they get there."

"It's a thought, though."

"It is, but it ain't a good one, Johnny. We come this far, we should thank the Almighty. Take what we can get, and count ourselves lucky to have it."

"I wish . . ."

"What?"

"Nothing . . ." He turned in the saddle and waved his hat to the drovers down behind him. He cut loose with a shout, and the men picked it up. The beeves started to push themselves a little faster, gaining momentum even on the long up slope. As they got closer, they could smell the water and drove themselves even harder.

Johnny rode on down to the river, leaving Rafe on the hilltop. The old man watched him urge his pony into the water. It was shallow for the first twenty yards, then grew suddenly deeper. Rafe could see by the swifter current in the center that the cattle were going to have a struggle getting across. Johnny was hanging on as his horse swam for the far bank. It was a good hundred yards before the pony touched bottom and another fifty before he climbed up on the grass across the river. Johnny was nearly a quarter mile downstream from his point of entry.

Every drive had a few steers who led the way in river crossings, and Rafe wheeled down to meet the herd. He collared Dan Harley and told him to cut the swimmers and get them up front, then made a wide sweep to the left. They were down to somewhere in the neighborhood of twenty-eight hundred head. But a loss of two hundred had to be considered a success. If the cattle brought anything like the prices they'd been hearing, they'd be in good shape as soon as they found a buyer.

Rafe found the tail end of the herd, a long, thin line of stragglers, and fell in behind them, shouting and waving his hat to force them up into the herd. If the cows were allowed to hang back, it would complicate the crossing and maybe cost them a few more head.

As the last of the reluctant beeves started up the incline, he heard gunshots. He strained to hear where they'd come from, but heard nothing over the cattle's hooves. Rafe charged up the slope, pausing just long enough to send Ralph Dalton back to drag ride. As he broke over the ridge, the leading edge of the herd was already in the water. The swimmers were out front a few yards, about to break into deep water. On the far side, he spotted Johnny, surrounded by a good dozen men.

Three hands had already started into the water, urging their horses across the river and drawing their guns. Rafe charged down the slope, afraid of Johnny's temper. All of them were frazzled, and it wouldn't take more than a wet match to light the fuse.

At the water's edge, Rafe leaned forward clinging to his pony's neck and braced himself for the water. He had closed the gap between himself and the other three, but once in the water, he had to be content with keeping pace.

Halfway across, he shouted to Johnny, but the bellowing cattle drowned out his voice. The first of the drovers was already in shallow water and Rafe shouted again. If they heard him, they showed no sign. Rafe drew his gun and fired into the air. The hands turned and he waved at them, shouting for them to hold up.

He couldn't tell whether they heard him or not, but they were confused enough to stand still until he was able to get to them.

"What in the hell's going on?"

Harley shook his head. "Dunno. A bunch of damn farmers come up out of nowhere. They fired a few times, and then Johnny started talking to them."

"You wait here," Rafe said. "No use spookin' them. Me and Johnny will handle it."

He dug in his spurs and his horse spurted up the bank. He dismounted ten yards behind Johnny and let the reins dangle while he joined his boss.

"What's the trouble, Johnny?" he asked.

"No trouble. Gentlemen, here, tell me we can't bring our herd across. Told them there was no way we wasn't. That's about where it stands." He looked at the farmers, several of whom were armed with rifles, the others with pitchforks and ax handles.

One of the farmers, a big, rawboned Irishman with hands like freckled grappling hooks, shook his head. The way the other farmers watched him, he must have been the leader. Rafe decided to treat him that way and see where it went.

"Gents," Rafe said, "name's Rafe MacCallister, from Baker, Texas. This here's Johnny Cotton." He stuck out a hand, but no one moved. Rafe shrugged, then continued, "We come a long way with them beeves. What do you expect us to do with them?"

The big Irishman shook his head. "Don't matter, as long as you don't bring 'em across the river. You can do what you want, otherwise."

"What's your objection, Mr. . . . ?"

"O'Hara, Kevin O'Hara. And the objection is them cattle are full of Spanish fever. You can lose half your herd without no problem. Most of us" — and he swept a hand out to take in his compatriots — "don't have more than a few head apiece. We lose them, we starve. Can't allow that."

"Listen, everybody's got to eat. Folks back east need the beef. We got it. All we want to do is drive the herd on to the railroad. What's the harm in that?"

Johnny was getting fidgety, and Rafe talked faster to keep him busy. "Be out of here in a day, two at the most."

"Can't allow it," O'Hara said. "Fact, there's a law against it. We can get the sheriff, if you want. He won't tell you no different."

"Hey, look," Johnny said. "This is a free country."

"No thanks to you, Reb," O'Hara said.

Johnny took a step forward, but Rafe grabbed his arm. "Now hold on, Johnny. Man's right. Maybe we should talk to the sheriff, see can we work this out peaceable like."

"Sheriff won't tell you nothing different," O'Hara said.

"Maybe not, but we'll wait here, all the same. You can send him out tonight, if you want."

"Sheriff's been in Abilene, won't be back till morning."

"Fine. Then you bring him out in the morning."

"We don't want any trouble."

"Neither do we."

"But we ain't afraid of it, neither. Man's got to protect what's his."

"We understand that. But you got to understand a coin's got two sides, Kevin. You got to look at our side, too. What's ours ain't dirt, it's beef, and it's swimmin' the river right behind us. It's what we got, same's your farms are what you got. Seems like we can work this out so's nobody gets hurt."

O'Hara seemed off balance, as if the unexpected proposition left him without options. "Wait here a minute," he said. Stepping away about fifty feet, the farmers conferred among themselves. They whispered, but the violence of the conversation told Rafe at least a few of them weren't satisfied with conciliation.

"Johnny," Rafe said, "you have to keep your pants on. These men are farmers, not Comanches. We can work this out, if you hold your water."

"I'm out of water, Rafe. All I got left is piss and vinegar."

"You want to get them steers through, you'll bite your lip. Let me handle things, will you?"

"This time. It don't work out, though, Rafe, and it's up to me from now on."

"Fair enough."

O'Hara returned with two or three of the other farmers. "You mind if we leave a couple or three men here with you? Make sure you don't try nothing?"

"You think we're liars, farm boy?" Johnny snapped. He took a step toward O'Hara, who outweighed him by a good thirty pounds and stood four inches taller, at least.

Rafe grabbed him. "Hold on, Johnny. The man don't mean nothing. He just wants to see we play fair. He don't know us from Adam's all he's saying."

"I know what he's saying. I just don't . . ."

"Shut up, Johnny." Rafe turned back to O'Hara. "Seems fair enough, Kevin. You leave whoever you want. You boys are welcome to eat with us, if you want."

"Now hold on, Rafe, we . . ."

"Johnny, I said shut up." To O'Hara, he said, "It's been a long trip. We're all a little short-tempered. But we'll work it out. A day's rest would do us all good, I reckon. Especially Johnny, here."

O'Hara nodded. "Alright then. We'll be back tomorrow, probably around noon, soon's the sheriff gets back. Don't expect him to tell you anything I didn't already tell you, though. We had the fever rip through here twice in the last four years. Tore hell out of the few cattle we have.

Oscar, here, lost near a whole herd of dairy cows."

Johnny snorted. "*Dairy cows.* Hell, man, no wonder. You might as well keep kitty cats or butterflies. What we got is sure enough Texas beef, tough as nails and mean as a grizzly."

"Maybe so, but what *we* have is what matters to us. You keep them cows down by the river until tomorrow."

Johnny shrugged. "Yeah, yeah, I heard you."

O'Hara delegated three men to stay, then he and the others trudged back up the hill behind them. A few minutes later, the cowhands could hear the creak of wagons as the farmers departed. Johnny laughed. "Christ almighty, damn *wagon* jockeys, no less. Rafe, I sure as hell hope you know what you're getting into. This don't work out, I might have to take up knitting."

"You just knit up them lips of yours for a few hours, and everything'll work out."

The three farmers kept apart, each of them sitting nervously with a rifle across his knees. The herd pushed on across the river, but Rafe strung pickets to make sure they didn't try to climb the ridge. When the last few stragglers were on the Kansas side, he gathered the hands and told them they were stopping for the night. Most of them took it in stride, although Dan Harley glanced at Johnny as if to ask why he was letting this happen.

As the sun went down, they sat around their campfire, conscious of the silent farmers on the hill above them, preferring to sit in the dark rather than join the cowboys for a meal. One of them kept jerking the lever on his old Henry carbine in what Rafe hoped was a nervous habit rather than a desire to use the weapon. The first shot fired, no matter by whom, would kill whatever chance there might be for compromise . . .

And they didn't need another setback. Not now, when they had come so far and were so close.

Johnny walked off into the darkness, down along the river. Rafe wanted to follow, but Johnny sent him back. "You can handle things, Rafe, so handle 'em. I need a little time to myself."

"You sure, Johnny?"

"Hell, Rafe, I'm not sure of nothin', no more."

The half-deserted spread weighed on Ted like a flat rock across his shoulders. Three months without a word from Johnny, and there was no hope of one, anytime soon. And every day, he went through the same routine. The small patch of vegetables he'd started reminded him of his brother. They had fought about it when he put it in. Vegetables were for farmers, Johnny said. Ted told him they were for eating, and Johnny had laughed. That had hurt, but it hurt even more now, thinking about it, and about how much he missed Johnny.

The summer was starting to fade now, not that it got any cooler, but there was a change in the air. Light looked different, colder, even though your skin couldn't feel the difference.

At least this night would be a little better

than most. He was having a quiet Sunday meal with Ellie and her father. He ran through the chores, making sure the horses were fed, putting a new shake wall on the shed behind the house. When he was finished nailing the shakes in place, he pulled a few splinters out of his fingers and stepped back to admire his handiwork.

The new wood made the rest of the place look shabby. He remembered houses like it, back in Alabama, where he was born. That part of his history was so long gone, it seemed like it must have been someone else's life. Something would jog his memory and he would stand there and look at it, the way he would a skeleton out on the flats. You'd see the bones, poke at them a little, try to picture what they looked like with meat on them, a little color instead of the washed-out gray-white of the skull and the rib cage, lying there like a barrel with every other stave missing.

Looking at the house was like that now. He didn't see the porch, he saw Johnny on the porch, swinging in the hammock. He didn't see the corral without imagining Rafe, one bony leg swinging up over the top rail to drop inside and break a new pony. Everyplace he looked, he saw pieces of a former life. It scraped away at him, like a block plane, slicing his skin away one curl at a time, always closer to the bone, and never long enough between passes to let him heal. He was an open sore, bleeding memory like water running down a sinkhole.

And Ellie tried to help, but she was no match for the past. He wanted to believe what she told him. But he suspected she was wrong. He wanted to believe, not because he agreed, but because it hurt too much to think Johnny might have been right. Something *had* gone out of him. He was changed, probably forever, and what mattered most was gone along with whatever else he'd lost.

When he'd finished the chores, he cleaned up and dressed carelessly. He'd been letting a lot of things go lately. Even Ellie had commented on it. She was right, but he just didn't give a damn. It seemed pointless to worry about little things when he couldn't do anything about all the big things that were wrong. That kind of logic made perfect sense to him, and after the third or fourth time she'd complained, even Ellie had stopped noticing.

He saddled his pony without paying much attention and let it find its own way to the Quitman house. The horse had no trouble, because the only places he ever went were to town and to visit Ellie. The horse took its own time, and Ted knew he was going to be late, but Ellie had gotten used to that, too.

When he rode into the front yard, she was on the porch, waiting. She ran one slender hand through her dark hair as she smiled at him.

"Been here long?" he asked.

"About an hour, I guess."

"Sorry."

"I don't mind."

"I would."

"If you would, then maybe you ought to pay more attention to the time."

"I thought you didn't mind?"

"I don't, but you said . . ."

"I know what I said, Ellie . . ."

The look she gave him stopped him in his tracks. "Sorry. I just don't think anymore."

"You can't let Johnny run your life from a thousand miles away."

"He doesn't."

"Yes, he does. Because you don't run it yourself."

"Are we going to go all through that again?"

"Not if you don't want to."

"I don't."

"Fine, then let's change the subject."

From inside the house, he heard footsteps. He glanced at the door just as Jacob Quitman pushed through the screen.

"Theodore, good of you to come, even if it is . . ."

"He already apologized, Daddy."

Jacob looked at him for a long moment. "I'm sure he did. But, it's not good to be wandering around with your head in the clouds. Not today."

"Why not?"

"It's not safe. Jack Wilkins lost a half-dozen horses last night. He thinks it was Comanches."

Ted glanced at Ellie, but she said nothing. He asked, "Is he sure?"

"He didn't see them, if that's what you mean. But he's reasonably sure."

Ted shook his head. "I was wondering when they'd come back."

"What do you mean?" Ellie asked.

"They don't like to lose. They lost two braves in the spring, during the roundup. They lost another just before Johnny left."

"The man he killed, you mean?"

Ted nodded. "The one I should have killed."

"No, son, you did right," Jacob said, patting his shoulder. "Violence doesn't solve anything."

"I used to think that. I still do, I guess. But . . . sometimes, I'm not so sure."

"Let's not talk about it, Ted," Ellie said. There was a hint of pleading in her voice. When he looked at her, she looked away. He wondered whether she might blame him somehow, but for what, he didn't know. Maybe she blamed him for not stopping Johnny. Or maybe she blamed him for not killing the Comanche himself. She seemed to agree with her father, but Ted wasn't quite sure. When she turned back, her face was calm, no hint of any contradiction.

"Ellie's right, let's have some dinner." Jacob stepped to the door and held it for Ellie. Ted waited for the old man, but was waved on in. He followed Ellie into the kitchen. Places were already set, and he could smell the pie cooling on the windowsill.

"Looks great," he said. "Smells even better."

"Ellie's a good cook," Jacob said. "She takes after her mother." His voice caught for a second, as if a word got stuck in his throat. He swallowed hard and looked away while Ted and Ellie sat down.

"Are you alright, Daddy?"

Jacob nodded. They both knew what was on his mind. Sarah Quitman had been dead for six years, herself a victim of the Comanches. Jacob didn't dwell on it, but there were little things that reminded him, unimportant in themselves, except for the memories they stirred.

"Maybe we should forget about everything and enjoy the meal, eh?" Jacob sniffed once, then picked up a carving knife to hack a few slabs of white meat off a roasted chicken. He speared them in turn and deposited two each on Ted's plate and his own, and gave Ellie one piece. "Eats like a bird herself, she does." He laughed.

Ellie chewed at her lower lip, then passed the vegetables.

"So, Theodore, have you given any more thought to what you want to do with your life now?" Jacob peered at him over the top of his glasses.

"Not really. I can't seem to make up my mind about anything these days."

"Maybe you have to forget about the past. Forget everything. You're a young man, with your whole life ahead of you. Someone my age, now, there's no hope. I am what I am, and, please God, that's good enough. But young people, they have choices. There's no mistake so great you can't set it right at your age."

"I wish I could believe that, Jacob."

"Oh, you can, son, you can."

They danced around the subject of Ted's future through most of the meal, never confronting it head-on, but saying nothing that didn't at least hint at the uncertainty. When the meal was finished, Jacob dragged him out on the porch. "Time for the men to talk about a few things, Ellie," he said. She smiled, but said nothing. If she felt excluded, she didn't seem to mind.

Outside, Jacob sat on a wooden rocker and Ted dropped to the top step of the porch. Jacob Quitman was a gentle man, but there was a strength in him that went beyond his size, which was just above average. The white beard made him look almost priestly, and the deep resonance of his voice just added to that impression. His powerful hands cupped in his lap, he smiled at Ted.

"I didn't want to say anything in front of Ellie," Jacob said, almost whispering, "but I'm afraid we may be in for some real trouble."

"The Comanches?"

Jacob nodded. "Aye, the Comanches. I

wish there was some way to convince them that Texas is big enough for all of us."

"I don't think it is," Ted said.

"You can't mean that. Why, this state is bigger than most countries of the world. How could there not be enough land for all of us?"

Ted spread his palms helplessly. "It was their land long before we were here. They can't forget that, and they sure won't forgive."

"At least you understand that. I'm not so sure about most of the people around here."

"I'm not so sure about me, either, Jacob."

"You can't blame them for trying to steal a few cows. I've been to their camps. Their children are undernourished, half of them. And with winter coming on, they've got to be concerned. That means we've got to be concerned, too. For them, as well as for ourselves."

"Jacob, you don't seem to realize that they don't give a hoot in hell, if you'll forgive the expression, about us. We're the enemy, plain and simple. They'd as soon as not scalp every last one of us."

"But like you said, Theodore, one can hardly blame them. They haven't been fairly dealt with. You know that as well as I do. None of the tribes has been."

"Tell that to Tommy Dawson. I nearly got him killed, trying to understand the Comanche. Would have, too, if Johnny hadn't been there."

"But Johnny's not here now. Now you have to think for yourself. All I'm suggesting is maybe a little understanding will go a lot further than another Indian war."

"Or another massacre?"

"I don't deny there's been violence on both sides, inexcusable violence. But nobody has tried anything *but* violence. Don't you see that?"

"Why are you telling me all this, Jacob? What's the point?"

"The point is, you're not like the others. Maybe you can make a difference."

"No, I can't. It's out of our hands. It's up to whoever's in charge upstairs, and I'm not so sure he's paying any attention."

"Never doubt it, son. If God had wanted man to take vengeance, He'd never have given him two cheeks."

"That's really a pretty sentiment, Jacob. I wish I could believe it, but I can't. You and Ellie, you're different from most of us. Maybe you're even right. My problem is, I just don't know. I've seen enough killing, that's for certain. But nothing else seems to work out here. There are too many people willing to kill you as it is. If they know they run no risk from you, it'll be even worse. I want to be like you, but I don't know how. At Shiloh . . ." He stopped abruptly and rubbed the corner of his mouth.

"Have you ever really tried anything else? Has Johnny?"

Ted shook his head. "Have you, Jacob? Have you ever thought what it might be like to find the Indian who killed your Sarah? Have you ever wondered what it would be like to look him in the eye and watch him understand the meaning of justice as your finger tightened on the trigger?"

"No, I haven't. You know that."

Ted sighed. "Yes, Jacob, I do know that. And I know you don't consider that justice. That's why I find it so hard to understand you. I want to be like you, but I don't know if I can."

"All you have to do is try, son."

"That takes more courage than I've got, I guess."

8

At sunup, Johnny had already been awake for an hour. He sat by himself on the hillside, watching the gray bulk of the herd slowly dissolve into individual lumps of color. As the red disc slipped one edge over the horizon, flooding the valley with red light, he could pick out the shapes of the night riders, half asleep in the saddle, watching the ends of the herd.

He glanced over his shoulder at the three farmers, who lay sleeping in their blankets. He envied them. They had something to protect, they knew what it was, and they'd be damned if they wouldn't do whatever they had to. He felt the same once, but now he wasn't so sure. The drive had already cost him a brother. And there was no end in sight. This latest wrinkle was just the least expected. He hoped it would be the last.

He watched Cookie light the fire and fill a big, ash-blackened coffee pot from one of the barrels on the mess wagon, then scoop coffee into the basket. After the coffee was on, Cookie looked up at the sun, then turned to scan the hillside. When he saw Johnny, he waved a hand, then turned back to breakfast.

Up on the hillside, Johnny heard the horses first. He yanked a pocket watch from his jeans. It was only six o'clock, too early for O'Hara and the sheriff. He started up the hill when a dozen riders broke over the ridge, reining in just past the crest. Whoever they were, they weren't the law. That much was clear.

Johnny sensed something he couldn't put his finger on. All twelve wore the tattered remnants of Yankee uniforms, mixed with CSA gray and whatever else had come to hand. There wasn't a clean-shaven face in the crowd of them. Several wore ammunition belts crossed on their chests, in the fashion of Mexican banditti.

Something told him not to get too close, and he stopped where he was. He knew better than to reach for his Colt, but he cast a quick eye toward his hip to make sure the gun was there. One of the crew dismounted, tossing the reins to a henchman and swaggering down the hill toward Johnny. He tucked his hands in his gun-belt, and his spurs clanked like he were proud of them.

He planted himself a half-dozen feet in front of Johnny, rocking back and forth on well-worn heels. Even allowing for the differential caused by the slope, he was a good four inches taller than the Texan.

"Cowboy?" he said as if it were Johnny's name. "You a long, long way from home, ain't you?"

"I been closer," Johnny said.

"I'll bet you have. That your herd down there?"

Johnny nodded.

"What've you got there, three, four thousand head?"

"More like twenty-seven hundred, why?"

Instead of answering the question, he turned to his cronies. "Man wants to know why?" he said.

The mounted men laughed, one even slapping his thighs in exaggerated enjoyment. The breeze quickened, and Johnny got a whiff of the wolf pack on the hill. He was ripe himself, but this went beyond the pale.

The big man stroked the ends of a full, ginger-colored beard, then scratched his jaw. "Seems like you need a little education. Texan, ain't you?"

Johnny nodded.

"Thought so. Cain't miss that drawl. I knew a few Texans my own self, once."

"Once?"

"Dead now. All of 'em. Secesh bastards, every last one. Kilt a few myself."

"The war's over."

"No it ain't."

"Look, if you just want to chew the fat, I got work to do."

"Chewin' the fat? Is that what I'm doin'?"

"Seems like."

"Maybe so, maybe it seems like it to you. But I got a different picture, see. I'm a tax collector, is what I am."

"Then don't let me keep you from your work." Johnny turned and started down the hill. He heard the spurs jingle and turned as the big man's hand landed on his arm. "Don't do that, mister."

"Don't you walk away from me, cowboy. Just don't, you hear me?"

"What I hear is a lot of hot air."

"You think it won't burn you, cowboy? That what you think?"

Johnny turned again. As he started down the hill, he spotted Rafe and two others sprinting toward him, carbines in their hands. Behind him, he heard several rifles cocked, and he turned back to the big man. At the same time, he waved Rafe off. If anything got started now, they wouldn't stand a chance. They were outgunned, and the big man held the high ground.

"What do you want from me, mister? I'm just trying to make a living, that's all."

"I already told you, I'm a tax collector."

"Tax collector? What kind of tax? I don't know what you're talking about."

"Then you better listen real good, 'cause I'm only gonna say this but one time."

"Go ahead." Johnny made no attempt to conceal his exasperation. It seemed to amuse the big man. He smiled broadly, revealing an uneven set of teeth the color of dead grass.

"You said you got twenty-seven hundred beeves, that right?"

"Yeah, that's right, give or take."

"Now, there you go. You got to give a little. I make it three thousand head, on the nose."

"What's the point, dammit?"

"I'm comin' to that. Just shut up and listen. Cattle are going for forty to fifty dollars a head over in Abilene. Seems like you're about to come into some pretty fat wallets, you and your hands."

"So?"

"If you get to Abilene. And if you still got them beeves when you get there. See what I mean?"

"No, I don't, and I don't really give a shit. Now, if you can't get to the point, I guess I'm gonna have to be rude and walk away. And this time, you put your hand on me, I'll rip it off at the goddamned elbow. You see what I mean?"

"So, a regular Texas wildman, are you? You gonna give me some shit about how you eat Comanches for breakfast and wash them down with half the Pecos River? 'Cause I got no patience for that kind of garbage."

"You do me a disservice, sir." Johnny grinned.

"That's more like it."

"Definitely. Because I wouldn't even give you garbage."

The smile on the big man's face vanished. His features seemed to contract and stiffen, like plaster shrinking as it hardens. When he opened his mouth again, there was a razor edge to his voice. "Now you listen to me, cowflop. You want to take them cows any farther, you got to pay. And that's a fact."

"Pay?"

"You heard me. Four dollars a head. At three thousand head" — he paused for a brief flicker of his former smile — "I make that twelve thousand dollars, U.S.A. money. Give or take."

"Are you crazy? Even if I was willing to pay, I don't have that kind of money. Twelve thousand dollars?"

"On the button, cowboy."

"No, sir, that just ain't in the cards."

"How much you got, then?" The big man seemed suddenly open to bargaining. But Johnny was not in the mood.

"For you, nothing."

"We can always take us some beeves, instead. Hell, you give me three hundred head, I can unload them in Abilene myself. At forty, it comes to the same thing."

"You're not as dumb as you look, are you?" Johnny asked.

"What do you mean?"

"You can do arithmetic just fine. Now try and understand some plain, old Texas English. No way, no time, am I giving you one dime. Nothing, you understand. No cattle, no money, nothing. And that's the last time I'm going to tell you. Now get out of my way."

This time Johnny didn't turn back. He heard the jingle of spurs, but he continued on down the slope. This time, Rafe and the other hands waited, their carbines pointed vaguely in the direction of the big man, who stood there with his mouth open, as if he didn't believe what had just happened.

As Johnny approached the bottom of the hill, Rafe jumped forward to meet him. "What in hell was all that about? What'd he want?"

"Said we got to pay him to bring the cattle through."

"*Pay* him?"

"Four dollars a head."

"What the hell for?"

"Said it was a tax. Permission to bring the herd through."

"Who is he?"

"Didn't say."

The three farmers scrambled down the hill to join the two men. Rafe glared at them, but they ignored him. One of the men grabbed Johnny's arm. "I was you, mister, I'd pay him."

Johnny whirled on them. "That part of your plan, boys? A way to put pressure on us, that what that was?"

The farmer who had spoken shook his head. "No, sir. He ain't one of us. Man doesn't know how to grow nothing. To him, crops are for burning. We have our own share of trouble with him."

"Then who in hell is he?"

"That was Ralph Conlee."

Johnny looked blank.

"Jayhawkers, mister, they was Jayhawkers. You rebels had Quantrill; Kansas had Jayhawkers. Still does."

"What's a Jayhawker?"

"A pirate in uniform, I guess. They started out during the war as irregular cavalry. Now, who knows what they are. All I can tell you is any one of them would as soon kill you as look at you. They take what they want. You'd best get your herd moving, better yet, give him what he wants, because he'll follow you until he gets it anyway, and he's not likely to settle now. You showed him up in front of that pack of wolves. He's sure not gonna forget it."

"What about the sheriff? He's still coming, isn't he?"

9

Ted sat on the ridge, looking down at the Wilkins spread. In first light, the place looked peaceful, almost deserted. Wilkins lived alone, and it was unusual for him to be asleep when the sun had been up for more than an hour. Nudging his horse down the steep grade, he angled across the slope. He froze for an instant when a glint of orange slashed past him. The burst of light momentarily blinded him, and he twisted away from it.

Looking through his fingers, he realized it was just a window, catching a few rays of sunlight. As he reached the flat, he kicked the pony once, then clucked to him. The horse broke into a trot, and he covered the last two hundred yards in short order. At the front of the house, he dropped to the ground, wondering where Wilkins was. It wasn't like the big man to ignore visitors.

He was supposed to have ears like a rabbit, and stories about his hearing were legendary. Most of them were almost certainly exaggerated if not outright false, but this still was odd.

Ted stepped onto the porch and rapped on the screen. He heard the echo of his knuckles, but nothing moved inside. He rapped again and turned to look across the yard, toward the barn and the corral. He wasn't even sure why he was here, but it was something he felt he had to do.

"Jack?" His voice seemed to bounce around the yard, then stop dead. Not even an echo from the barn. He rapped a third time, then pulled the screen open. He tried the door, and it swung open easily with a press of his fingers.

"Jack? You in there?"

Wilkins still didn't answer. Ted felt the hair on the back of his neck prickle, a sensation he hadn't had in three years, not since he'd left the front as the war was winding down. Inside, everything looked normal. He went to the bedroom and stood in the doorway.

The door was half open, and Ted could see the lower half of the bed, but it was empty and, from the looks of it, unslept in. Wilkins never took pains with the ordinary domestic details, so there was no way to be sure.

The bedroom was empty. Ted shook his head and walked back to the front room, which tripled as kitchen, dining room, and living room. Wilkins had planned to add another room, but when his wife, Mabel, caught typhoid, he hadn't bothered. When Mabel died, there was no reason. Jack's Winchester was missing from over the fireplace, but it was the only thing out of the ordinary.

Ted stepped off the porch and crossed to the barn. The barn door was open, and he walked through cautiously, convinced that something was seriously wrong. Jerking his Colt free, he ducked to the left, just inside the dark barn.

"Jack, you in there? Jack Wilkins?"

His own voice came back at him, and something skittered across the loft, but no one answered him. Rather than search the barn on his own, he thought about riding for help, then pushed the idea aside. If Wilkins needed that much help, it was already too late for him.

He backed out of the barn and walked around to the rear. On the way past the corral, he noticed rails were down on the back side. On the damp ground, he spotted half a dozen moccasin prints. They could have been from the day before, but he didn't think so. A little water still sat in the center of each depression. If the prints were a day old, there would have been no such puddles.

Ted stared off through the stand of cottonwoods behind the barn. Then, for some reason he didn't understand, he raced toward the trees, as if something were drawing him there against his will. The hair on his neck was standing out straight, now.

"Jack?"

Again, he got no answer. Pushing into the sparse undergrowth, he saw a smear of blood on some leaves. There was no mistaking it. It was fresh and glistened in the sun as the leaves rippled in the breeze. On the far side of the brush, he found Jack's Winchester.

He picked it up and sniffed the muzzle. The sharp bite of gunsmoke told him the carbine had been fired recently. So there was hope the blood wasn't Jack's. Hope . . . but not conviction.

Ted started out into the saw grass, where he saw another smear of blood. A few yards ahead, he saw flies swarming around the tips of the grass blades. He sprinted for the spot, found even more blood, and a place where the grass had been pressed flat, probably by a human body. The long oval depression was smeared with fresh blood, and the flies were already busy.

He moved slowly now, brushing the grass away with his forearm. The grass was bent in a long, narrow channel winding off toward the creek bed another hundred yards away. An occasional smear of blood glittered on the grass. So far, there was no sign of Jack or anyone else. No sign, that is, except for the blood. It could even belong to a horse, but he didn't think so.

Ted straightened, cocking his ears toward the gentle slope across the creek. He might have heard something, but wasn't sure. He knew he didn't want to go any farther on foot. If someone was out there, he couldn't risk being run down by a mounted man, whether white or Indian. He sprinted back to the house, Jack's Winchester cradled in his arms.

Dashing into the house, he grabbed a box of shells for the carbine from the ledge over the fireplace, then ran back out to his pony. He sprang into the saddle and urged the horse around the barn. He picked up the trail almost where he'd left off, and slowed the horse to a walk. Keeping one eye on the ground ahead and one on the channel through the rough grass, he followed the pattern of bloodstains with mounting concern.

Down by the creek, he stopped and dismounted. The marshy edge of the creek was covered with prints, all fresh. Hoofprints and the depressions of moccasined feet intermingled. There was no doubt now that Jack Wilkins had had a second visit from the Comanches. The only question was, where was Jack?

Little swirls of mud eddied in the water, silt curling just above the creek bed, clouds of light brown in the clear water. He looked upstream, then remounted. The pony didn't want to go, and he squeezed it with his knees until it stepped into the tepid water.

Fifteen yards later, he was sorry.

Jack Wilkins lay on the creek bank, his hands bobbing in the sluggish current. His throat had been cut, and his scalp was gone. For good measure, a lance had been driven through his belly, pinning the body to the ground. Ted turned away, his stomach churning, a bitter fluid rising from his gut and filling his mouth with the taste of metal.

Torn between the desire to run away,

and the need to do something about the horrible vision oozing the last of its blood into the sand, he kneed the pony ahead a few paces. The horse tossed its head and shied away from the body. Ted didn't look, couldn't look, and swallowed hard.

He took a deep breath, then jerked his canteen from the pommel and took a long pull on the warm water. He swirled it around, trying to wash away the taste of his own bile, and spat into the creek. He shuddered once, then took a second long swallow from the canteen. It changed nothing.

Pulling on the reins, he pushed the pony up onto the far bank. Ted followed the course of the stream, leaning far over to look for some sign that the Comanches had left the water. It was not uncommon for someone trying to elude a tracker to use a streambed to double back, but the little mud eddies seemed strong enough a lead to pursue them upstream.

He didn't doubt they were paying the white man, any white man, back for their recent losses at the hands of the Cotton men. In one sense, he was directly responsible for the bloody corpse lying back there. And part of him wanted revenge. He could hear Jacob's voice as if the old man were riding at his side, warning him that revenge was not the way, but he wanted it anyway. Jacob wasn't there, after all. And besides, what could Jacob know about the guilt he felt?

The creek flowed a little faster as he started uphill a little. It was only two more miles to the spring where the creek had its source. If he didn't find anything by then, he'd have to make a decision. If he tried too long and too hard to do it on his own, he was helping the Comanches make their getaway. But if he was close now and went back to town, he'd be doing the same thing.

Plunging ahead, he was only too aware, was exactly what Johnny would do, but that made it all the more important for him to push on. It seemed almost as if he were filling in for his absent brother, doing what Cottons had always done.

It was pigheaded, and he knew it, but he also knew he had no choice. Part of him was withering away, and if there was any way to stop it before it had gone too far, he had to try. For all he knew, it was already too late. But he didn't want to spend the rest of his life wondering when, or if, he had stopped being a man, at least the way the Cotton family had always defined it.

He was less than a mile away from the

spring now, and still hadn't seen a sign. The stream was narrowing perceptibly. If the Comanches' raiding party had come this way, they would have had to have gone in single file in another quarter of a mile. That would be no problem, except for the fact they were driving stolen horses. Unless they had them on a string, keeping them in line would have been all but impossible.

Fifty yards later, it didn't matter anymore. He found the place where they'd come out of the water. Half a dozen unshod Indian ponies and nearly a dozen more wearing iron shoes, Jack Wilkins's remaining horses, had climbed up the bank, leaving water-filled prints in the short span of soft sand between the water's edge and the verge of the saw grass. Not more than two hours before, probably more like one, the horses had passed this way. He followed the bent grass for three miles before he realized they were headed for the mouth of Breakneck Canyon.

It was almost too neat.

It was coincidental, more than likely, but there was a kind of fitness to it, too, one that he recognized and that the Comanches would appreciate. They were going to have another go at it. But this time he was on his own.

This time, though, he was not going into the canyon. This time, he would take the long way around and ride the rimrock. If the Comanches were taking the short route on through, he'd have an advantage, maybe offset the odds a bit. If not, at least they would have only the advantage of numbers. The high ground would be neutral.

He worked the switchbacks in a hurry, almost jerking the reins too hard at every hairpin. The loose rock beneath the pony's hooves skidded and skipped away, bouncing like flat stones on a summer pond, but he didn't worry about it. The Comanches weren't stupid. They had to be expecting pursuit. If they had wanted to stand and fight, he'd have run into them long before now. It seemed obvious they wanted to put as much distance as possible between themselves and the scene of the small massacre that had been Jack Wilkins.

No longer the scourge of the Texas plains, they were still a fearsome enemy. But they seemed to realize their days were numbered. The battle at Adobe Walls had taken a heavy toll. Superior in numbers, the Comanche had been outgunned and had their spirit crushed by Kit Carson's men in the rooms of Bent's trading post. Most of the Comanches had long since surrendered and accepted the imposed tranquility of the reservation.

But by no means all.

And, as usual, it was the most fearless who refused to be confined. As far as Ted could tell, this was no hit-and-run band who would scurry like frightened squirrels to the reservation and prop one another's spirits in the middle of the night with reminiscences of the raid. These were free-ranging Indians, wild red men, avatars of an earlier time.

He'd know for certain when he found them.

10

It was past midday, and Ted was beginning to wonder if he had made a mistake. Halfway across the rimrock ledge of Breakneck Canyon, he still hadn't seen a single sign of the Comanches. In a couple of hours, he'd have to start thinking about going back. There was no way in hell he would spend the night alone on the rim. Not even a madman would risk that.

And Jacob Quitman's voice still whispered to him, telling him how foolish he was being. Only God can make that kind of decision, Theodore. Not man. Man has no right to judge his fellows, not the way you are doing. And when a man tries to pass judgment on another culture, he is trespassing all the more on alien territory. He flies too close to the sun, and he gets burned. That is a law of nature. It is, even more, a law of God, Theodore.

Or so Jacob would have it.

The first blush of his rage long since faded, reason was crowding him, nudging the passion aside, making him wonder why he was there at all. He wondered, but deep down he knew the answer. It was one he didn't like, so he chose to wonder still, in hopes that there might be some other, still hidden, reason.

And in the other ear, Johnny kept shouting, trying to drown Jacob out: "You yellow bastard . . . you yellow bastard." And Ted knew he wouldn't be there at all unless he at least half believed that Johnny was right. He was trying to prove something to himself, and to Johnny. It didn't seem to matter that Johnny wasn't even there, and might never know what he'd been trying to do.

He could die out here, and when somebody stumbled over the gleaming cage of his ribs, another rack of bones on the dry-as-dust rim of the canyon, no one would know who he had been, or what his name was. And no one would care! Bones were all too common out here. The irony was that bones had no color. A Comanche and a white man, stripped of flesh and sinew, looked the same. After death, the same wind whistled through the white pipe organ, playing the same monotonous song for Comanche and Texan alike.

And Ted Cotton wondered whether that was all he had left. Maybe that's how he wanted it to end. Maybe he was even right to want that.

Maybe.

But he'd never know; not until it was too late to change his mind.

As he neared the far end of the canyon, he heard something far below him. Almost certain it was a horse, he dismounted. Creeping close to the edge of the rim, he took cover behind a jumble of rocks. Cocking an ear, he strained to hear it again. After a long moment, it drifted up to him, the shuddering whinny of a horse.

Then, metal struck rock, and he knew it was a shod horse. Creeping even closer to the rim, he leaned out to look down into the canyon. Almost directly beneath him, several horses, on a string, shuffled nervously. As he tried to get even closer, one hand slipped on the sandy rock. He landed hard on his elbow, dislodging a chink of stone. He reached for it, but it skittered away from his fingertips and disappeared over the rim.

Ted pressed himself flat, waiting an eternity before he heard the rock land below.

The horses nickered, and he heard one or two of them paw at the ground. It was almost as if they sensed something, even at this distance.

He was breathing shallowly, his throat constricting and the air whistling noisily down into his lungs. His mouth was dry, and he tried to moisten his lips with his tongue. The rasp sounded like emery paper and left them as dry as they had been.

A whiff of burning wood drifted up from below. The Comanches weren't waiting for him, they were pitching camp. They'd never have risked a fire if they thought someone was on their trail. That tipped the odds a little in his favor. But not much. He repositioned the hand and levered himself up again. Wrapping one leg around a rock, he slid closer to the rim. With his hat off, he peeked out over the rock straight down nearly two hundred feet.

There was no sign of the Comanches. His skin went cold. Maybe they *were* aware of him. Maybe this was all a decoy, while they slipped up behind him. He was suddenly paralyzed. It wasn't fear. It was that sudden flash of understanding. Life was more complicated than he was willing to see. This wasn't about life and death, exactly. It was more about the way the two intersected.

The seamless web of connections. Ted and the Comanche he'd killed, Johnny and his dead Indian, Jack Wilkins and the red man who'd lifted his scalp. And now this, just the latest intersection, one of many, each as meaningless as the others, or as meaningful. It all depended on how you wanted to look at it. And what paralyzed Ted Cotton was not knowing. What the hell was he supposed to do? What should he think?

He lay there, stunned by the depth of his confusion. And the silence saved his life.

The whisper of leather on stone, so soft he would have missed it if he had been breathing normally, made him turn. The Comanche stared at him for a second, then leapt. Ted rolled aside, and the Indian landed heavily, just to his right. The charge carried the Indian to the edge of the rimrock, and the slippery sand prevented him from stopping.

The Comanche shouted and Ted turned as he started to go over the edge. Instinctively, Ted grabbed for him, catching the Indian by one knee-length moccasin. The Indian pitched over the edge and Ted braced himself for the shock. He arrested the fall, but the Comanche was already out of sight. The soft leather felt smooth under Ted's fingers, the brave's weight ripped at his shoulder socket.

Wrapping his legs around a rock, Ted squeezed with his thighs and crooked both knees to lock them in place. Rolling partway over, he was able to get his free hand on the same ankle. He ignored the searing pain in his shoulder and reached out over the edge, groping for something to grab onto, shifting his grip and latching onto the Comanche's leather leggings.

The Indian squirmed as Ted inched forward. Almost close enough to the edge to look over the rim, he gritted his teeth. Hauling on the leg like a fisherman, he scissored his legs, dragging himself back a few inches. It grew quiet. His elbows scraped the rock, sand whispering between stone and bone as he dragged the Comanche back.

The brave's left leg swung up and over the rim, and Ted pulled harder. The pressure eased a bit, and he realized the Comanche was pushing away from the rock face with his arms in some bizarre push-up. The Indian's hips were almost level with the ledge now. It made pulling easier. Under the soft leather, Ted could feel the hard muscle and the harder bone beneath it.

"Hold on," he shouted, not even sure the Indian spoke English. He felt silly, but didn't know what else to do. "Stay still. I'm going to change my grip."

The Comanche seemed to understand. He lay quiet, and Ted squeezed harder with his right hand, digging his fingers into the legging and curling them. Reaching out as far as he could with the left hand, he latched onto another fistful of leather and pulled. The Comanche's hips scraped toward him, and he could see the man's head now, swiveled to the right.

The black eyes staring at him over the red man's shoulder seemed confused. Terror was there, but it was mixed with something else, some lack of understanding, as if wondering why this white man hadn't let him go. Was it only to preserve him for some other form of death? The thought flashed through Ted's mind like a meteor, that this man, whose life he held, literally, in his hands, might have been the one who drove the lance into Jack Wilkins. Maybe it was his knife that had skinned Jack's skull.

For a second, he thought he should let go, let gravity avenge Wilkins. It wouldn't, after all, be his fault if the Comanche couldn't fly. The Indian seemed to sense his thinking, and for a moment, the confusion in the black eyes was gone. There was nothing there but terror, terror that turned to an icy calm. Then that, too, was gone, and there was hatred for an instant, pure unadulterated hatred, and then nothing. The black eyes were suddenly empty. Just blackness, deeper than anything Ted had ever seen.

And he held on.

Straining with every muscle, Ted hauled the Comanche back several inches, then stopped to catch his breath. He dug his teeth into his lower lip and pulled again, far enough for the Indian to raise up on his knees. Ted lay there panting. For the first time, he realized his shoulder hurt from more than the strain. He brought a hand up as the Comanche turned toward him, pivoting on his legginged knees.

Ted felt the slit in his shirt, the sticky blood soaking the severed edges. At the same instant, he saw the knife in the Comanche's hand. He grabbed for his Colt as the Comanche curled the corners of his mouth in what might have been a sardonic smile. The brave waved the knife, its broad, flat blade catching the sunlight and sparkling for a second, then he stuck the knife into its buckskin sheath and stood up.

Ted felt the sweat on his palms. The Colt was slippery in his grip as he backed away, scrambling on his hips. The Comanche shook his head, the slightest nod, and Ted turned to see two more, watching him. The Comanche stepped toward him, reached down with one hand, and hauled Ted to his feet. Then, without a backward glance, he stepped past. A moment later, all three Indians were gone.

He sat there on the rock, wondering what it all meant. Had the Indian suggested they were even? It couldn't have been more than that, certainly. It could have been less. A life for a life, it seemed to say. Or did it?

Ted got to his feet and dusted himself off. His shoulder had begun to throb, and he squeezed it closed with one hand, squeezing his Colt in the other. He heard the horses below for a moment, then nothing.

He was all alone on the lip of the canyon. He looked up at the sun. It was already beginning to turn red, slipping low on the horizon. His shadow, tinged with orange at its edges, speared out from him as he turned his back to the sun.

Walking back to his horse, he took several deep breaths, trying to purge himself of the fear and the confusion. The horse backed skittishly as he approached. Snatching at the reins, he got the pony calmed down. Ted clapped a hand on the pommel and hauled himself into the saddle. As he settled in, he felt something against his leg, something that shouldn't be there. He looked down. Then, realizing what it was, he leaned over the side and threw up.

Dangling from a rawhide thong was a bloody scalp that could only belong to Jack Wilkins.

When his guts stopped churning, he realized the Comanche had settled accounts. All bets were off now, and the next time, if there was a next time, they were even. The slate was now clean, in a way even the Comanche did not understand.

He wondered what Jacob would think, if he told the old Quaker what had happened. He wondered whether he would tell him anything at all. He prodded the pony with his knees, turning back toward home.

And he knew the answer to both questions.

11

Ellie sat on the grass. Her skirt spread out around her legs, she patted the ground alongside her. Ted shook his head. "I'd rather stand," he said.

"You have to put it out of your mind."

"I can't."

"You did the right thing."

"How?"

"Would it have brought Mr. Wilkins back, if you had killed that man?"

"Of course not, Ellie, but that's not what I mean."

"But it *is* what you mean. You understood it, even though you don't understand *how* you understood. But that doesn't matter. There has to be another way. People can't kill one another until there is only one man left alive. What would be the point?"

"It would leave the planet for the fish

and the birds. There's something to be said for that, maybe."

"Only as long as you can't accept that God intends us for better things. But we have to be ready for them. It can't happen until we are, because He won't allow it."

"God was not on that ledge. I was. It was me who grabbed that Comanche and pulled him back, not God."

"But they could have killed you. You told me so, and I believe it. You have already made a difference. That Indian will remember what you did for the rest of his life."

"It won't change him none."

"You don't know that."

Ted didn't answer. He bent down to snag a fistful of grass and stuck a long blade between his lips. Finally, unable to stand the pressure of her expectant stare, he shook his head. "No, I don't know that. But it doesn't change anything."

"It changes everything. That's the whole point. You're different now, not like Johnny, not like the rest of the men around here. You know you don't have to pick up a gun every time someone looks at you cross-eyed."

"I don't know that."

"Yes, you do."

Ted walked to the edge of the spring and squatted down. He swept at a water skimmer with the ends of the grass, then watched as the long-legged bug sailed across the surface until it was out of reach.

The sun on the pond hurt his eyes, and he squinted across the water to where Jacob, his back bent under the bright light, hacked at the ground with a hoe. Row by tedious row, he'd been slashing at the hard-baked soil, then crawling on hands and knees to plant seedlings.

As he finished the latest row, he straightened to mop the sweat from his face and neck. He took his broad-brimmed hat and fanned himself a few times, then glanced over to where Ted and Ellie were sitting. When the old man noticed Ted watching him, he waved before dropping to his knees and going back to the planting.

"I think I ought to give Jacob a hand, Ellie. That's too much work for one man."

"It's honest work, and he doesn't mind."

"And what I do isn't honest?"

"I didn't mean that. He wants to do it, even though it's not easy. He gets pleasure from it."

"I just meant that it was hard on a man his age."

Ellie didn't answer and he looked over

his shoulder. She was staring at the ground.

"What are you thinking about?"

"I was just . . . never mind."

"Come on, tell me."

"It was nothing, really. Just woolgathering, I guess."

"You won't make a sheepherder out of me, if that's what's on your mind." He laughed, but she took him seriously.

"Actually, I was wondering what you were going to do. If Johnny doesn't come back, I mean."

"Johnny's not coming back. He made that pretty plain."

"Then what *are* you going to do? You can't keep that ranch going by yourself."

"It's not much of a ranch, really. But it *is* our land. My daddy's buried there. I can't leave."

"Johnny did."

"I'm not Johnny," he snapped.

"My point exactly."

"Don't try to confuse me."

"You seem to be doing that pretty well on your own."

"What do you know about it? It's easy for you. You know what you think, and you see what you want to see. You wouldn't change if a thousand men died in front of your eyes. And you're a woman, to boot."

"You noticed."

"What's that supposed to mean?"

"I don't know. Forget I said it."

"Look, I'm going to help Jacob. We'll talk about it later."

"You run away from the wrong things, Ted."

"I'm not running away."

"No? Then what do you call it?"

Ted stalked off without answering. He skirted the pond, then cut through the tall grass and out into the plot of baked earth. It felt like stone under his feet, and he wondered not only how Jacob could work it by hand, but why.

As he drew close, he tried to smile. "Need some help, Jacob?"

The old man stopped to lean on his hoe. "Always need help, Theodore. It seems like this ground resents my attempts to cultivate it."

"That's cow country for you. Stubborn, ornery."

"Cowmen, too, I think."

"You mean me?"

"Not only you. I've been watching you two. Anything wrong?"

"You'll have to ask Ellie."

"I'm asking you, Theodore. You can say

what's on your mind. Plain speaking is my preference, you know."

"So I see." He looked off at the sky for a moment before answering. "I don't know. I guess me and Ellie just don't see some things the same way."

"I sometimes think that's what God wanted. It gives husbands and wives something to do on winter nights."

"What's that?"

"Argue, what else?" He laughed, and it sounded like the joy of a man half his age. His whole body shook, and his face split into a broad grin. "You should try it sometime."

"I don't know if I'm cut out for that, Jacob."

"My Ellie thinks you are."

"Maybe not anymore."

"Trouble? I don't mean a spat, I mean real trouble?"

Ted shook his head. "I don't know. I guess so."

"You can work it out."

"I'm not so sure we can, Jacob. We're so different. I don't know if either one of us can change."

"Of course you can. Both of you can. It's hard work, but nothing worth having comes easy."

"We'll have to see." He pointed at the seedlings. "What do you want me to do?"

Jacob turned to look back toward the house. "You see those two buckets, by the well?"

Ted nodded. "Yeah."

"You can water these plants. Not too much. I don't want them to get used to too much water. But a little, just so the roots take hold."

Ted walked toward the house, stepping carefully across the rows of plants. At the well, he snatched the first bucket and hooked it on the well rope. Lowering it down, he listened for the splash as the oak hit the water, then waited a few seconds for it to fill before cranking it back up. He filled the second bucket and lugged them both back toward the garden.

Water sloshed on his ankles and soaked his pants from the knees down. The pails were large and heavy, but after a half dozen trips, it began to feel good. He settled into a rhythm. Each row took four pails, and Jacob already had nine planted before Ted even got started.

Jacob's work was harder and more time-consuming, and Ted offered to switch off, but the old man shook his head. "This is something you have to grow into, Theodore. Planting things and helping them grow takes patience. It's not like anything you are used to."

"I could learn."

"I'm sure you could, but not today. Today, I want to get everything planted. Next spring, I can show you. Time won't be so precious then. We can go slowly, and make sure it's done right."

"If you change your mind, let me know."

"I will."

They finished the work without more conversation. Jacob hummed to himself, in a rich baritone that quavered as he hoed, rose and fell as he leaned over to plant. Ted watched Ellie as she moved past the garden. She skirted the far edge of the staked plot without speaking, then walked to the house.

He wanted to say something, but decided to take a page from Jacob's book. Patience, as alien to him as to all Cottons, hurt a little, but he bit his tongue and kept on working. When Ellie was gone inside, Jacob stopped for a minute to stretch his back. He groaned as he bent his shoulders back, his hands on his hips.

"Not so young as I was, Theodore."

"You want to switch?"

"Not so old as that." He smiled, then got

to his feet. "Time to water something besides the seedlings, eh?" He moved toward the well, with Ted right behind him. Both men were sweating, and Ted's shoulders ached from the constant pull of the heavy pails. He was used to hard work, but he was using muscles he seldom bothered, and they resented it.

At the well, Jacob lowered a pail, then tugged it back up without using the crank. He took a hammered metal dipper and scooped water into it, rinsed his mouth, and spat. "I guess you are used to dust, the same way I am."

Ted nodded.

"It's so much drier here than Ohio. I hadn't expected that."

"This is hard country."

"I am a hard man, Theodore. I will win, you wait and see."

"I hope you do, Jacob. I sure as hell hope somebody around here wins something. And soon."

"No need for profanity, son."

Ted didn't answer. He'd spotted something on the horizon, beyond the spring. He took a step toward it, shielding his eyes from the glare.

Jacob noticed. "What is it?"

"Not sure, Jacob. A rider, comin' hard,

but I can't tell who it is."

He broke for the house at a run. "Come on, Jacob, come on." He turned to see the old man staring off at the approaching rider. He called again. When it was clear Jacob wouldn't follow, he sprinted toward the house at full speed. He burst inside. "Ellie? You here?"

"What's the matter?" She came out of the next room, unfolded clothes in her arms. "What's wrong?"

"Maybe nothing. I just wanted to make sure you were inside."

"Where's my father?"

"He's still in the garden. He wouldn't come. Just stay here."

Dashing back through the door, he rounded his pony and grabbed his rifle. The rider was still coming flat out, and had narrowed the gap considerably. Ted ran back to Jacob, who scowled at him when he saw the gun. "No need for that," he said.

"I hope you're right, Jacob." The rider was outlined by the cloud of dust his horse was kicking up. But his face was just a blur in the bright sun.

As the rider drew closer, his horse started to look familiar. Less than a quarter mile away now, he still lashed his mount with the reins, driving the pony as hard as he could.

"Looks like Rafe," Ted said.

"That couldn't be," Jacob said.

But it was. And it could only be bad news.

When the old cowboy was close enough, he jumped from his pony and walked the last few steps.

"Rafe, what the hell is going on? Why aren't you up north?"

The old man shook his head. He looked exhausted. The creases in his leathery skin were caked with trail dust. Even through the beige coating, Ted could see the dark circles and the bags under Rafe's eyes.

"Teddy, I got some bad news. Awful bad news."

"What happened? You lose the herd? Where's Johnny?"

"That's what I come to tell you, Teddy." He paused and looked at Jacob for a moment. "Johnny ain't with me, Teddy. He's dead."

"What?"

"Dear God," Jacob muttered. He walked heavily to the screen door, opened it, and leaned into the house. "Ellie, you better come out here."

Ted swallowed hard. He searched Rafe's

face for some evidence that this was just a cruel, misguided prank. There was none.

He turned and walked away, leaving the messenger confused and alone in the front yard. Walking down toward the spring, he stared into the water for a long time. One thought kept running through his head. "It's my fault," he whispered. "It's my fault."

12

Ted and Rafe sat on the front porch. Jacob and Ellie had left them alone. For a long time, Ted didn't say anything, and Rafe waited. The questions were there, but he wasn't anxious to try and supply the answers. None of them would really change anything.

As the sun started to sink, Ted got up and walked back and forth on the unpainted boards. His spurs jingled, and the sound was almost too musical, too cheerful. Ted didn't seem to notice, but it was driving Rafe crazy. He kept quiet because it was Ted's grief, not his own, and he had no right to make demands of any kind.

When Ted finally spoke, there was no trace of the kind of razor-edged anger he'd expected. Johnny would have stewed until he exploded. Ted was different. He seemed calm, almost too calm.

"What happened?" he asked.

"We never seen it coming, Teddy. Johnny was all set for the sonofabitch. But he fooled us."

"Who? Who fooled you?"

"Ralph Conlee. I dunno. I had a bad feeling, but Johnny thought we were alright. Them farmers warned us, so it shouldn't have been no surprise. But it was though. It surely was."

"Rafe, just make it plain and make it short. No hedging. I want to know exactly what happened. That's all I want to know. Tell me, dammit."

Rafe sighed. This was what he was afraid of. But there it was, and there was no way to avoid it. Not now. He could have sent one of the other hands, but that would have been too easy, and Rafe was no coward. "Jayhawkers, Teddy. Some damn kind of Yankee irregulars gone to seed. No better'n damn savages, you want to know the truth of it. They wanted money to let the herd pass. We didn't have none, of course, least not near enough to what they wanted. Then they wanted a piece of the herd. Johnny was mad by then, and told them no."

"You know for sure who did it?"

"Sure as I can be. I was there."

"Go on."

"We thought we was free and clear. We sneaked the herd away from Meshaw, this little town just across the Arkansas River. And . . ."

"Sneaked? Why?"

"Because the farmers didn't want us there neither, Teddy. They got no use for Texas cattle nohow, say they got some kind of fever kills their own stock. I dunno nothing about that, but that's what they told us. They was the ones stopped us in the first place. We was waiting for the sheriff, to see can he get them to let us through. But Conlee showed up first. I think, really, once that happened, it was already too late. You have to see this man to believe him. Like a creature from hell, he was, smelled so bad I liked to throw up. They was all that way. Like maybe water would kill them or something. Anyhow, once Conlee latched on, you could see it might happen. Come to shootin', anyways."

"But . . . ?"

"But we was goin' to try and snooker 'em."

"What about this sheriff?"

"What about him?"

"What'd he do?"

"Not a damn thing, Ted. They got him

buffaloed. He don't say it, but I think he's scared of Conlee. Acted like it, anyhow. They all are. Them farmers didn't think nothing of staring us down over them Winchesters and hayforks they was carryin', but they got no stomach for Conlee. That's what made me think we were in for a bad time. I tried to talk your brother into leavin' right away, but he wanted to wait for the sheriff. Then, when Sheriff Mitchell showed up, he said he couldn't do nothing about Conlee, anyhow. So we waited for nothing."

Ted stared off at the deepening purple. A mass of clouds, pink at the edges, swirled across half the sky. He kept running one hand through his hair, sometimes tugging at it, sometimes raking his fingers across his scalp so hard Rafe could hear the nails digging into the skin. But he didn't say anything for nearly a quarter hour.

Ellie poked her head out to ask if they wanted coffee, but Rafe waved her off. Ted wasn't half done yet, and Rafe knew it. Ellie nodded and backed away from the door. Ted never looked around, not even at Rafe.

"That's a fine young woman, there, Teddy."

Ted said nothing.

Not knowing what else to do, Rafe continued, "That night, we thought maybe we fooled them, threw them off the scent, so to speak. Johnny wanted us to stay up all night in shifts, not just the night pickets, but half the hands. Half would sleep a few hours, then spell the others. We done that, too, but nothing happened. Not that night. And not the next night, either. During the day, we sent two man teams back to see if we were bein' followed. Nobody ever saw a sign, but they must have been there all along. It was their country. They could almost guess which way we'd have to go, and we walked right into it."

"Into what?"

"The plain truth?"

Ted nodded. "The plain truth."

"It were a Sharps buffalo gun got Johnny. He never had a chance. Sonofabitch kilt him from near half a mile away. He didn't suffer none, thank the Lord. We buried him right there that afternoon. A pretty little spot, really. In a stand of pines."

"Where?"

"About eighteen, maybe twenty miles outside of Triple Steeple, another little town. Got three churches, though. That's how it's called that."

Ted got up and stepped off the porch.

"Where you goin', son?"

"Home, Rafe. I got some work to do."

"I'll come with you."

"No, you stay and have some supper. You had a long ride."

"I can wait, Teddy."

"I'd rather be alone a bit, Rafe. Sort some things out."

Rafe nodded. "I'll be along in a while."

Ted mounted his horse and wheeled away from the house. Rafe watched him disappear into the dark, then got up and went inside. He explained what had happened to Jacob and Ellie. Ellie wanted to run after Ted, but the men wouldn't let her go. She screamed at them and carried on, even slapping her father for the first time in her life, but Jacob just held on for dear life until the tantrum passed.

The two old men were quiet, Rafe preferring not to think about what had happened, Jacob preferring not to think about what was almost bound to happen next.

Ted looked back once. The house seemed quiet, lamps throwing a warm orange glow through the trees. But the blackness of the night slowly swallowed the house and its light, leaving him alone. He rode slowly, not really in a hurry, and dead certain he would get where he was going.

As he rode up a ridge, he caught one more glimpse of the house, just above the treetops, then he passed the crest, and it disappeared altogether as he started down the far side. Out on the plains, coyotes howled at one another and at the feeble moon. He was tempted to ride out into the vastness, thinking maybe they weren't coyotes at all, but Comanches come to taunt him in his grief. But that was too unrealistic, and he realized it.

Soon, the coyotes fell silent, and he heard nothing but the sound of his pony's hooves on the hard-baked earth and raspy saw grass. When the house came into view, he slowed even further. At first he wasn't aware of it. Then when he realized it, he understood why immediately. It was the first time he'd enter the house knowing he was alone in the world. As remote as the possibility had seemed, he had still believed there was a chance that Johnny would come home. Now there was no way he could believe that.

It was over. His life was over. His future was over. He was a man with a past and nothing else.

He didn't go in right away, preferring to linger outside on the dark porch, as if waiting long enough might give whatever passed for God in this new and lonely world time to change his mind. History might be like a stream, and if God were as powerful as men like Jacob believed, He could direct its waters anywhere He chose, even make them double back on themselves, send them off in some new direction. That was what God was for, wasn't it?

He shook his head, realizing he was twisting a notion he didn't even accept. There was no God. There couldn't be. He had no brother, how could there be a God?

Taking a deep breath he reached down inside himself for the courage to face the unalterable. Once the door opened, it was written in stone. Johnny was dead and he wasn't coming home. Not ever. He stopped with his palms pressed flat against the splintery wood then; knowing delay was pointless, he shoved the door back. It creaked on its hinges, and one board scraped against the floor as it had for months, wearing a smooth, bone-white arc in the floorboards.

He groped in the dark until his fingers closed over the chimney of a coal oil lamp. The box of matches was right next to it on the old table he and Johnny had made for their father fifteen years before. The table had never been useful, but his father had refused to let it go. When John Cotton died, Johnny claimed it for his own, and was, if anything, even more protective of it than his father had been.

And now it was all that was left. He removed the chimney and struck the match. The flame surged, almost died out, then came back a bit. He touched it to the blackened wick and waited for the oil to catch fire. When the flame was steady, he replaced the chimney and walked to the fireplace. An oval needlepoint hung over the mantel. His mother had made it just before taking sick.

Ted read the motto, stitched with the rough, bold hand of a woman who had met a hard life on its own terms. "Bless this house." That was the motto, in blue letters surrounded by a garland of red and yellow flowers. The colors of the threads had begun to fade, and the white linen had turned ivory. Soon it, too, would be gone.

Like the woman who made it. Like the man who loved her. Like the first son she'd borne him. All gone, and for what?

Ted sighed, then collapsed in the rickety wooden rocker Johnny kept by the fireplace. He cried for the first time, and it all came out of him at once. The loss of his brother, the terror of Shiloh, the fear on the rim of Breakneck Canyon. Everything that had ever terrified him poured out in a soundless flood. He wanted to shout, to scream defiance at someone or something, but he couldn't.

There *was* no one to scream at.

He sat there all night, rocking back and forth, listening to the squeak of the floorboards under the chair. The rhythm was somehow comforting.

Rafe stuck his head in at one point. Ted sensed him, but didn't acknowledge him. The old cowboy withdrew and went to the bunkhouse.

And when morning came, Ted watched the sun come up. It spilled through the windows, leaking in around the curtains and crossing the floor toward the chair like a transparent flood. He could feel its warmth on his shins as the cotton turned the light to heat. When it had climbed across his lap and down the other side, he stood and walked to the window.

He listened to the birds for a few moments, then went to the bedroom where he and his brother had slept. He was almost packed when he heard footsteps on the porch. He heard a knock and saw Rafe at the door.

"I got to go back, Teddy. We still got most of the herd. Somebody's got to see to it. I been gone near a month already."

"No, Rafe."

"But . . ."

"I said no! You stay here, watch the place."

"Where are you going?"

"Where do you think?"

"But you can't, Teddy."

"But I can't not, Rafe."

The old man nodded. "You be careful, son."

"No, Rafe, I won't." Ted's voice was cold and hard. "But I'll be back, all the same."

13

Ted rode like a man with the devil on his ass. Covering fifty and sixty miles in a day, he stopped at nightfall, ate a meal, and slept like a dead man. At sunup, he grabbed breakfast, climbed back into the saddle, and didn't stop unless he had to. He had one spare horse and switched them daily. Riding right up the belly of the heartland, he blew through Arkansas, threading his way through the Ozarks, and climbed into the plains.

Three weeks later, he reached the Kansas border. For the first time since he'd left, he camped before sundown. When the fire was built, he sat on a hilltop and watched the waters of the Arkansas roll by. Flecks of foam in the dying light danced like fire. High overhead, a hawk, almost too high to see, drifted on the wind, flapping its wings every few minutes to change direction or loft to another current. It was a windy evening, and there was a chill in the air, but he ignored the fire halfway down the slope. He sat there until the sun went all the way out.

He was close now and the worst was just ahead of him. The hot rage that fueled him all the way from Texas was gone. In its place, an icy calm settled in his gut. The tremors were gone, the sudden tic of an eyelid or twitch of a cheek, frozen by that calm, no longer troubled him. It seemed almost as if getting here were more than half the battle. He knew that wasn't true, but he had been driven by the fear that he would never even get to Kansas. That would have been a failure worse than anything he could imagine.

Now there it was, sitting across the river. Its rolling hills had faded with the sun. In the twilight, it had looked like a landscape of gray ice. Now, in the darkness, he couldn't see it at all.

But it was there.

And somewhere in its belly was the man who had killed his brother. But the calm had its insidious side. With it came time for reflection. He knew Johnny would commend him. He also knew that Ellie would never forgive him. And he was right back staring at that same blank wall again. What should he do? Should he avenge his brother, or listen to the woman who loved him?

And did it make any difference?

Ted knew that he could be dead in a week. If that happened, it might be a blessing. No matter which way he chose, he would never have to choose again, never have to face himself in a shaving mirror with that question mark between his eyebrows, never have to wonder if he had made the right choice. The need to choose would end with his life. That knowledge gave him some sort of perverse pleasure.

He would rest now. Tomorrow he would begin the search. Closing his eyes, he leaned back against the chilly ground and waited for sleep. He could feel the frozen knot beginning to chill every nerve in his body. Each limb felt as if it were sculpted from ice. Ted wondered if he had ever felt this calm. It brought him back to the night of April 4, 1862. He had lain on another hillside then. And like now, there had been no fire. The Yankees were out there then. Snipers swarmed all over the woods, tying themselves in trees and just waiting for some fool to pass between a roaring fire and a gunsight. It hadn't taken long to realize it was better to be cold than to be dead.

At least that's what he had thought then. But he was young, and life had seemed like it would never end unless he made a mistake. And he had been too young to make mistakes. He was no longer that young. And he was no longer that naive. The next day had stripped him of whatever innocence he had.

It came back as plain as day, the way it always did. There had been rain. Everyplace he looked, there was mud. Sometimes the troops had to sleep in fields so full of standing water, they were no better than swamps. The roads, tramped on by hundreds of horses and thousands of men, turned to rivers of thick, clinging clay. The wagons bogged down time after time and often had to be manhandled to get them free of the morass.

For days, there were skirmishes. Cavalry patrols would run afoul of pickets. Musket fire would crack for twenty minutes, then one side or the other would withdraw, dragging a couple of wounded men, hurling curses over their shoulders. No one had any idea of the horror that was to come.

It seemed then almost like a picnic with

fireworks. Now and then somebody got hurt, but that happened at picnics, too. The guns were toys. After all, the troops were children, most of them. It was the officers who were the old men. Old men leading boys into a cauldron full of molten lead that would scald the flesh from their bones and leave them gasping like dying fish on the muddy ground.

It started by accident, and Ted wasn't even there. Most of the officers were surprised by it, and almost all of the men. But it didn't take long to turn from a schoolboy's outing to a hellish nightmare. The cannons fired canisters full of grape shot, balls the size of small plums, then exploded and scattered the deadly shot in every direction. Limbs were torn off, leaving stumps spouting blood in thick gouts. Eyes were lost, hands and arms and legs blown away.

One of Ted's friends, a kid who couldn't have been more than sixteen or seventeen, got shot through the belly. Ted knelt beside him where the blood on his uniform almost obscured the foot of intestines ripped through the wound by the minié ball. The kid kept screaming, and Ted could do nothing but slit the wound a little and stuff the intestine back. Then he sat there and held the kid's head in his lap until he died.

All day and into the next, it continued. Men fell on both sides by tens and hundreds. He never did learn how many died. But the smell of the gunsmoke, so thick it hung like a lowering fog over the fields, was still with him.

And it was to get worse before it was over. A charge with fixed bayonets into a Federal camp, almost on the banks of the Tennessee River, was the last straw. Sweeping through the tents, firing at things that moved and things that didn't, they burst open the camp, stabbing at wounded men who were too close to death to do anything but lie there and feel the cold steel again and again slice through their bodies.

And the men wielding the bayonets were men he slept and ate with, men he sang with at nights. They were his friends. They were just like him.

And it made him sick.

It was then he started to wonder. He didn't sleep much for the next three years. Every time he closed his eyes, he saw the kid holding his gut, then the eyes closing, as the kid died. One officer, his arm blown off by a Federal battery, stared at the bloody stump every night in his dreams, the uninjured hand waving in the air where the other arm had been, as if he couldn't believe his arm was no longer there.

So damn long ago, he thought, so damn long ago that it must have been someone else asleep on that earlier hill. That was where it had all started. And this is where it had led.

And the pictures flashed through his mind one after another. Things he could not forget, and things he did not want to remember. Whenever it happened he tried to force himself to look somewhere else. There were so many things he remembered barely at all. Memories flitting just below the surface, like trout darting under sunny water, hiding in the glare, slipping into the shadows, teasing him with a curve here, a faint flick of a tail there. And as soon as he would cast for them, they were gone.

It would be better to remember nothing at all, than to remember only those things he could remember. Once in a while something would tease him. Some smell would carry him back to Alabama for a moment. His mother would be in the kitchen, flour up to her elbows, a checkered apron knotted around her waist. But as soon as he tried to focus on it, it would be gone. It was like he were a criminal, teased by the things he couldn't have. Pounding on the bars got him nowhere. He could look, but not touch.

And tomorrow would begin one more of those strings of memories he was condemned not to forget. Where it would lead was anybody's guess. That it would end violently was certain. That someone would die was probable. That it might be Ted Cotton seemed like a blessing.

As he finally drifted to sleep, he felt like he were flying. His body seemed to lift off the ground. He felt the wind carry him along like the hawk he had been watching at sundown. He could see all the way to Mexico, and the tips of mountains he'd only heard about flashed in the sun.

Then everything went black, and he was falling. He fell forever, but he wasn't afraid. He didn't tense up, waiting for the impact of his body on the ground. He knew, without having to think about it, that it might never happen, and if it did, he knew it wouldn't hurt.

He woke up just as the sun came up. Rubbing his eyes, he watched the red light in the east fade away. It grew white, and he could no longer bear to look at it. Even the water of the Arkansas turned white as milk.

As soon as he felt the sun's warmth on his skin, he walked downhill and rebuilt his fire. The last of his coffee went into the pot, barely enough to make a cup, but it would have to do. Gnawing on a hunk of dried beef, he waited for the coffee to brew, then washed the salty taste of the meat down with the scalding liquid.

Kicking the fire out, he saddled his pony and secured his relief horse to the saddle horn, using a longer rope than usual for the crossing. Swinging up into the saddle, he felt light, almost cheerful. Whatever lay ahead of him was something he had to confront. The sooner the better, he thought.

As his pony eased into the river, he braced himself for the first burst of current. The pony started to swim, straining to keep its head above the swirling waters. He could feel the animal reaching for the river bottom, its legs churning like windmills.

And when he got close to the opposite bank, the pony exploded out of the water, as if frightened of something beneath the surface. Ted looked back, wondering if he would live to cross it again. Then, as if Texas were someplace he never expected to see again, he turned away from the south and kicked the pony up the slope. He wondered where the herd had crossed, and tugged Rafe's map from his shirt pocket. He'd examined it so many times, it was falling apart at the creases. Mud-stained, some of the pencil marks rubbed away by his fingertips, it could barely be read in spots.

But he was close now, and in a day or two, he'd no longer need it at all. There were no maps leading to Ralph Conlee. He'd have to find the bastard on his own.

But he was ready.

He *would* find him.

14

The first task was to find the herd. According to Rafe, the hands were going to camp in the area until Ted decided what to do. Rafe had negotiated permission from the sheriff, on the condition that the beeves be kept under close guard and not allowed to wander freely. The farmers had been unhappy with the decision, but they had agreed. Conlee's raiders had visited more than a little grief on them, and Rafe thought they harbored the secret hope that somehow, working with the cattlemen, they could rid themselves of the scourge once and for all.

A mile from the river, Ted hit a road and headed west. So far, he had seen no sign of human life, no fences, no tilled fields, no buildings of any kind. There was only the road, which started on the eastern horizon, in the middle of nowhere, and stretched out toward another nowhere in the west.

When he'd gone four miles, he spotted a plume of smoke ahead. It appeared to be just off the road, and he broke his pony into a trot. A half hour's ride brought him in sight of a chimney. As he continued on, a roof rose above the flat ground, hovering like a platform in the air. Slowly, the roof rose and the house beneath it appeared. Ten minutes later, he could see a fence, running straight off the road, and he galloped toward it.

Turning into a narrow lane, lined with split rails on either side, he approached the house, not knowing quite what to expect. A barn, fifty yards from the house and surrounded by trees on three sides, sported a large railed pen, in which he could see half a dozen horses.

Beyond the barn, a fenced field contained more than two dozen head of the strangest-looking cows he'd ever seen. Instead of the long, lean lines of the Texas longhorns, these animals were blocky, more like buffalo than cows at all. Reddish brown with white faces, he thought they might have been built to the blueprint of a child's crayon sketch.

He entered the broad yard, slowing his horse as much out of uncertainty as courtesy. A figure appeared in the barn doorway. The man ducked inside for a moment, then reappeared with a shotgun and ran toward the house. By the time Ted reached the hitching post by the porch, the man was planted in the doorway, the shotgun none too casually aimed in his direction.

"Howdy," Ted said. "Mind if I get down?"

"Depends on what you want."

"Information, mostly. And some fresh water."

"Water we got. Information, maybe."

Ted slipped from the saddle. "Mind if I tie up?"

"Long as you don't knot it."

Walking toward the porch, Ted held out his hand. "Name's Ted Cotton."

"Cotton?" The man seemed to relax a little. "Texas, right?"

Ted nodded. "That's right. How'd you know?"

"You Johnny's brother?"

"I was, yes." Ted swallowed hard.

The man on the porch shook his head and let the shotgun rest on the floor, butt first. "That was a damn shame, Mr. Cotton. I sure am sorry."

When Ted didn't answer, the farmer said, "Kevin O'Hara's my name. Come on inside. You must have had a long ride. Seems like Rafe didn't leave that long ago."

"You met Johnny, then?"

O'Hara nodded. "I did. I wish things could have worked out different. But . . ."

"They will," Ted said. "I can promise you that."

"You don't mean you're gonna take Conlee on, do you?"

Again, Ted was silent. O'Hara turned to step through the door and held the screen open for Ted to follow. Inside, Ted saw a large room, with a big wooden table and a coal stove in one corner. Half a dozen chairs lined the table, three on either side. "Have a seat, Mr. Cotton. Let me get Millie."

O'Hara disappeared through a doorway hung with a blanket, and Ted could hear low voices beyond it for a moment. O'Hara reappeared and pulled a chair out from the table. "Have a seat. Millie will be right out."

O'Hara dropped into a chair, and Ted sat across from him. The farmer looked at him directly, as if he were trying to place him in memory somehow. "You favor your brother a bit. He was bigger, but . . ."

Ted shook his head. "It's alright. I don't mind talking about it."

O'Hara sighed. "I should have seen it comin', but everybody here was so worked up about your herd, all we could think about was ourselves."

"I gather Conlee is a problem for you folks, too."

"Problem? Oh, yeah, you could say that, but it don't go half far enough. He's got everybody on the border for two hundred miles in either direction shaking in his boots. Good reason, too."

"Why's that?"

"He's a savage, worse than any Indian. The man has no shred of human decency or compassion. He doesn't just take what he wants, he kills who he wants, and tortures people for the fun of it. Why, not three months ago he . . ."

O'Hara stopped when he heard footsteps just beyond the suspended blanket. "Here's Millie."

A slender young woman, her sandy hair pulled back in a bun, stepped through the doorway and smiled. "Mr. Cotton," she said, "would you care for something to eat?"

"No, thanks, I just . . ."

"Come now, you must be hungry, and it must be weeks since you've had any decent food."

"Don't want to be any trouble, ma'am."

"No trouble, I assure you." She didn't wait for him to argue any longer. Turning her attention to the stove, she got a fire going under a huge iron cauldron. "I made this soup this morning. I just have to heat it up."

O'Hara watched her fondly. "No point in arguing with Millie. She gets a fire under her, there's no turning back. You're bound to eat something whether you want to or not."

Ted smiled. "I guess I better get my bib, then." He laughed. "Now, Mr. O'Hara, what were you about to tell me?"

Millie canted her head slightly. O'Hara noticed and shook his head. Signaling with his eyes that he didn't want to talk in front of Millie. "No need to bother about that right now. Plenty of time to talk. Listen, I got to finish up in the barn. Care to give me a hand?"

"Man ought to earn his keep," Ted said, pushing back a chair.

The men walked outside and O'Hara glanced back once or twice at the house, as if to make sure that Millie hadn't followed them.

Once they entered the barn, he turned to Ted. "I don't want Millie to hear any of this. She's already nervous about being out here. What I'm gonna say would just make things worse."

"It's that bad, is it?"

"Worse. The sheriff's a good man, but we might as well be without the law. Conlee and his animals know nobody will help Tom Mitchell. They can go anywhere and do anything. Not just around here, but all up and down the border. There's not enough law. The army don't seem to care. Maybe it's too much trouble for them, or maybe they worry too much about the wrong kind of savage. I don't know. But what I *do* know is that Conlee has to be stopped. But I don't know how."

"He will be."

"Can you count on your hands?"

"I don't know."

O'Hara seemed surprised at the answer. "They seemed to worship your brother. I would have thought . . ."

"They did worship Johnny. But they're not so sure about me." Ted debated whether to tell O'Hara about the last few weeks in Texas, before Johnny had come north with the herd, but decided there was no point in it. "Johnny was always the boss. Cowhands are funny. They don't transfer loyalty so easy. Just because you're related to the boss doesn't make you the boss. You got to earn their trust. I haven't. Not yet, anyway."

"I wish I could tell you folks around here would pitch in, but I can't."

"What about you?"

"What about me?"

"Will you pitch in?"

"I don't think so."

Ted shook his head. "No wonder Conlee gets away with murder."

"Look, Ted, you have to understand something. Conlee is like a force of nature around here. He was here before I got here. He'll be here long after I'm gone, most likely. But as long as I'm here, I got to *be* here. You can just saddle up and ride away. You get him riled up, he won't chase you but so for, because he knows this area, and he knows the people. It makes him feel secure. But if you get him riled up, he'll take it out on somebody, whether you're here or not. That means me and folks like me. Our whole lives are here. We *have* to stay."

"If you call it a life, letting somebody like Conlee keep you scared of speakin' your mind, scared to stand up for yourselves, then I guess you're welcome to it."

"Look, Ted, I can understand you being

angry, disappointed even, but that's the way it is. I'd be lyin' if I said it wasn't. But look at it from our point of view. Hell, it was your brother he killed, among others. If Johnny couldn't beat him at his game, how can you expect a bunch of farmers to do it. Hell, I never even saw a gun until we packed up to move out here, much less own one. Even now, I don't know whether I'd trust myself to use it. I can stand up to any man in a fair fight, with my hands. But that's not what this is. This isn't hands, and it sure as hell ain't a fair fight. Unless you get that through your head, we might as well get your headstone ready, right next to your brother's. Because that's what it'll come to."

"Look, O'Hara, I'm not here to make the world safe for nobody. I'm here for one reason, and one reason only. Ralph Conlee killed my brother. I think he ought to pay for it. If I can do anything to make that happen, then I'll do it. I don't care how, either, as long as it happens."

"You might as well figure on working alone. If your boys help out, you still got a chance, but not much of one. I reckon some or most of you boys were in the war. But Conlee's got hisself a unit. That's the difference. They're used to workin' together; they know they can depend on one another. That gives them a big edge, mighty big. You want to buck them odds, you go right ahead. But don't look to nobody around here for help. Like I said, I wish it could be different, but it ain't. And it won't never change, as long as Conlee is around. Maybe, if he had come after we were already here, it might've been different. But the fact is, he was already tearin' hell out of the countryside before most of us got here. We either didn't know about him or didn't care. Either way, it's his countryside, not ours."

"You seem to think he's not human, like he can't be hurt, can't be beat."

O'Hara shook his head. "You got that right. You ever seen some of the things he done, you'd think the same. I seen three men, brothers, their heads on a row of stakes, like goddamn pumpkins. I saw a woman slit from chin to belly, laid open like a trout. And that was only after they were done with her. You can imagine the rest of it. He's killed more'n a half-dozen children I know of. You ride out of here fifty miles in any direction, you see a burnt-out wreck of a farmhouse, a barn turned to cinders, you can bet it was Ralph Conlee lit the match. If he wants somethin', he takes it. If he don't want it, he makes sure it ain't no use to nobody else. Butt heads with him, you get yours broke. And your neck to boot."

Ted was quiet for a long time. When he finally broke the silence, he whispered, "I still got to do it. I can't let him get away with it."

"It's your funeral, I'm tellin' you, Cotton. It's your funeral."

"Maybe so, but I'd rather die tryin' than walk away knowin' I didn't give a damn. I couldn't live like that. Not for long, anyhow."

"Folks do what they got to."

"Not always, O'Hara, not always."

"Mr. Cotton's right, Kevin."

O'Hara whirled. "Damn it, Millie, how long you been sneakin' around out there?"

"Long enough."

15

"It's over the next hill," O'Hara said. "Or should be, anyhow."

He looked uncomfortable, sitting his horse as if it were a wagon. Ted felt sorry for him, but was angry at the same time. How could a man with so much to lose be so damned cautious, he wondered. Couldn't he see what he was doing?

It was none of his business, but it made him mad anyway. And he knew that what lay ahead of him would be a little easier if he could have convinced O'Hara, and the others like him, to throw their weight to his cause. They had the same cause, after all, but as long as O'Hara refused to see that, Ted knew he might as well be hollering down a rain barrel, for all the good it would do.

As they broke up the slope, Ted nudged his horse a little ahead. He could hear

O'Hara trying to convince his horse to keep up, but the big Irishman was no cowboy, and no horseman either.

Ted broke over the ridge, expecting to see the herd placidly munching at the rich Kansas grass. What he saw instead almost made his heart stop. Instead of three thousand beeves, he saw three, maybe four hundred.

The chuck wagon sat to one side of a broad meadow, a plume of smoke spiraling up from a rather tentative-looking campfire. He spotted a couple of the hands on horseback, keeping the meager herd under control, but they were underworked. It wouldn't have taken three kids on hobby horses to ride herd on what was left.

He almost came to a dead halt, stunned into granitelike immobility. He waited for O'Hara, turning in the saddle to watch the farmer cover the last two hundred yards. When the Irishman was abreast of him, he reined in. The look on his face was somewhere between sheepish and sorrowful.

"What in hell happened to my herd?" he asked.

"I don't know how to tell you," O'Hara said. "Figured it would be better if you saw for yourself."

"You mean to tell me Conlee made off

with nearly twenty-five hundred head of cattle?"

O'Hara nodded. "That's right."

"Thanks for your help," Ted said. "I'll take care of it from here."

"You sure you don't want me to wait around?"

"For what?"

"Yeah, I guess you're right." O'Hara struggled to get his horse to turn back down the hill. "You know where I am, if there's anything I can do."

"Thanks," Ted said. He tried to keep the edge out of his voice, but didn't think he succeeded. When the farmer was gone, he charged down the hill, making straight for the mess wagon. He didn't wait for his horse to stop, jumping off after tugging on the reins. The animal seemed confused to lose its rider so suddenly, and pawed the ground right behind him.

Cookie poked his head around the wagon. He made a quick stab at a smile, but it went nowhere. "Figured you'd be here before too long," he said.

"Cookie, what in hell happened to the herd?"

"Oh, you mean them cows we nursemaided for near two thousand miles. That the herd you mean?"

"Damn it, you know what I'm talking about."

"Well, we ain't got too much left. Hung on to what we could. Hands and beeves, both. But we're scrapin' bottom, Teddy."

"Conlee?"

" 'Bout right. Sumbitch run 'em off a few hundred at a time. Never could stop him. Never knew when to expect him. He had us outgunned anyhow. And after Johnny . . . well, that kind of took the tar out of the boys. Lot of 'em left right afterward. What we got left ain't much to look at, and I reckon they'd have run off too, if anybody'd have 'em. Which I surely doubt."

"How come you hung around?"

"Thought somebody ought to stay and tell you what happened. Didn't reckon anybody else would, so . . ." The old man shrugged.

"I don't know whether to thank you or tell you what a fool you are."

"You can do both, I think. Seems like I got both comin'. You want some grub?"

"Nope."

"What are you fixin' to do . . . to get even, I mean."

"Don't know."

"You *are* fixin' to get even, I hope. Else I hung on fer nothin'."

Ted didn't answer him. Instead, he turned to look at the sorry remnants of the herd. Cookie tugged on his sleeve. "I didn't, did I?" When Ted turned, he continued, "Hang on fer nothin'?"

Until that moment, Ted didn't know the answer. But there was no way to avoid it now. "No," he whispered, "you didn't hang on for nothing."

"Good. I didn't think so. You might be a mite slow, but you *are* a Cotton. Seems like you and me are the only ones who didn't fergit that."

"Thanks, Cookie."

The old man reached out to squeeze Ted's forearm. Then, without asking, he turned to the triangle suspended over the tail of the wagon and started rapping it with a metal spoon. The bell, ordinarily so welcome, seemed somehow feeble with so few cattle, and so few men to tend them. The hands wandered toward the mess wagon, three on foot and three on horseback.

They gathered around like schoolboys staring at a new teacher, wondering what new tricks they'd have to invent to get by.

The oldest of them was no more than twenty, and probably short of that by a few months.

"I guess you boys must be tired of hanging around," Ted said.

They looked at one another, but said nothing.

Ted continued, "Anybody wants to collect his wages, you let me know. I brought enough cash to settle up with everybody. Since most of the hands are gone, I guess I can pay a bonus for anyone who wants to leave, and raise the pay of anyone who wants to stay."

"What's the use of stayin'," one of the younger men asked. "We got no damn herd."

"That's true. But we can get it back."

"Not likely," the kid continued.

"It won't be easy, I know that. But if you're game, so am I."

"Johnny couldn't hang on to it. How in hell you expect to get it back?"

"Johnny's dead, Buck."

"Hell, I know that. Fact is, he was the only thing holdin' us together. The older guys run off, but I need the money. That's the only reason I stayed. I don't have no desire to get my head blowed off. Not for no damn cows."

Ted nodded. "Alright. How about the rest of you boys? You all feel the same way?"

"Reckon we do, Mr. Cotton," another of the kids said. He couldn't have been more than seventeen. "I get my pay, I guess I'll head on back to Texas. I don't like it here."

"Can't say I blame you, Peewee. But . . ."

"No buts, Mr. Cotton," Buck said. "We never even figured you to be here. Figured Rafe would come back with our pay."

"Why didn't you think I'd come?"

"Hell, you know why. So's ever'body else. Ain't no secret."

"It is to me . . ."

Buck looked for support to the other hands, but they were busy looking at the ground, watching their toes scratch blunt lines in the dirt. He hitched up his belt and sucked his teeth for a moment. "I was there in Breakneck. Maybe you forgot about that, but I didn't. And I know sure as hell Tommy Dawson didn't. You like to got him killed. Some of us figure you *did* get Johnny killed."

Ted felt as if he'd been punched in the gut. "You bastard," he said, taking a step toward the kid. "You lousy bastard."

The kid reached for his gun, but Ted was too fast for him. He stepped in and landed a quick combination, driving Buck back on his heels. The kid had to bring his hands up to protect his face, but he was just a hair too slow. The right cross nailed him on the jaw and he went down hard. Ted stood over him, breathing through his teeth. "Get up, you sonofabitch. Get the fuck up!"

Ted felt Cookie wrap his arms around him. He struggled to break free, but the old man had powerful hands, and he locked them together like a vise, then dragged Ted back three or four steps. "Settle down, Teddy. Settle down. The kid don't mean nothin' others ain't been whisperin' behind their hands. Least he had the guts to say it out loud."

Ted finally broke free. He turned on Cookie, who backed away a step and held up his hands. "Hold on, son, don't go poppin' at me."

"You're all a bunch of lyin' bastards," Ted shouted. He stalked to his horse and dug into his saddlebags. A moment later, he pulled out a thick canvas bag with a drawstring. Untying the knot, he reached in and tugged out a fistful of bills and coins, threw the whole thing in the air, then walked away. Climbing into the saddle, he watched the hands scramble for the money, his tongue between his teeth.

"We're even. You come up short, talk to somebody who come up long. I don't ever want to see any of you again."

"No need to worry about that, Cotton," Buck said. "Conlee'll peel your hide back and make a damn rucksack out of it."

"We'll see about that."

"Oh, I know it." Buck laughed. "You know, Cotton, I was your brother, I'da shot you, 'stead of that Comanche. Done a whole lot more good."

Ted pulled his Colt and cocked the hammer. Buck backed up a step, but he didn't look frightened, just disgusted. "I thought you had the guts to use that, I reckon I'd be scared. But . . ."

Ted fired once, and the bullet tore through the edge of Buck's left boot. The kid danced on one foot, cursing at Ted and grinning. "Crazy sonofabitch. You ought to have your head blowed off. I reckon Conlee can handle it, though."

"Sure as hell know you can't, Buck," Ted said. "Now get out of here before I drill you a third eye."

Buck danced away, reluctant to put his full weight on the foot. He wasn't hurt, but this time he was scared. Ted didn't blame him, he was frightened of himself, wondering whether he would shoot Buck or if it was all just some crazy bluff. Not knowing was the scary part.

"Teddy," Cookie said, "I don't think that was such a good idea."

"I liked it."

"You got enough troubles without turnin' ever'body agin you. You can't handle this by yourself. You know it and I know it."

"No, Cookie. I don't know it. In fact, I think I have to handle it by myself. I think that's the only way *to* handle it."

"I sure hope you know what yer doin'."

"Me, too, Cookie. But I'll tell you one thing. If I don't, it ain't gonna matter a hell of a lot."

16

Ted scoured the countryside for three days, looking for some lead to get him on Conlee's trail. Cookie stayed on, and he used the old man as a touchstone. They camped beside the mess wagon, after cutting the cattle loose and hauling the wagon about four miles to a nearby creek. Summer was dying quickly, and Ted was only too conscious that the first snow would be due in two months, at the outside.

On his daily forays, he saw the kind of evidence O'Hara had warned him about. Ruined homesteads, burned to the ground, sometimes rock chimneys the only things left standing. Barns turned to ashes. And always, the ashes were cold. He had found plenty of evidence of Ralph Conlee, but not a single clue to his present whereabouts.

He was beginning to feel like he was

cursed from the outset. He lay awake half the night nearly every night, wondering if he'd ever get a chance to make it up to Johnny. It seemed strange to lie there, seeing his brother's face so clearly, and knowing that he'd never touch him again, never slap him on the shoulder or shake his hand. He wished he'd had a chance to say good-bye, but that wasn't in the cards. He thought about asking Cookie to take him to the grave, but he wasn't sure he could stand it.

He needed every ounce of energy to concentrate on the work at hand. If he allowed the past to distract him, he might meet Johnny again a whole lot sooner than he'd care to. And Jacob paid him a visit now and then, looking like some avenging angel, wagging a finger under his nose. The old Quaker's voice, deep as thunder and wavering like some ghost in a play, terrified him. It was so real, he'd wake up talking to Jacob, asking him what to do, or arguing with the old man, explaining how Johnny wouldn't rest until Conlee paid for what he'd done.

But in the morning, it was deathly still. There was never a footprint in the dew, never a bent blade of grass. He'd been alone, as he knew he had, but . . .

And Cookie kept an eye on him, the way Rafe had always done. He'd try to teach him things without lecturing. Sometimes Ted listened, and sometimes he saw through the old man's intention. When that happened, he'd pretend to listen, to spare Cookie's feelings. He wasn't sure he was getting anywhere, and there were times when he felt that he might just as well be locked up in a jail cell somewhere. He found walls no matter which way he turned.

But on the fourth day, he got lucky. Smoke on the horizon brought him at a full gallop. It was no cooking fire. The smoke was too thick for that, and too black. It rolled up like a small thunderhead, then spread out on the wind. Something big was burning out of control.

He cut across the plains at an angle to the road, trying for the most direct route. As he narrowed the gap, he heard gunshots. A second funnel of smoke ballooned up alongside the first. He broke over a gentle rise, and he could see the flames, a hungry orange licking at the bottom edges of the black smoke. A house and a barn had been torched.

Charging down the slope, he saw horsemen, as many as a dozen, burst through the smoke and head toward the road. He was close enough to hear the pounding hooves now. A couple of gun-shots cracked from somewhere behind the smoke, but the riders ignored them.

Ted was torn. Obviously, someone was still alive, somewhere in the middle of the inferno. He didn't want to lose the trail of the raiders, but he couldn't let anyone stay in that raging holocaust. He charged for the larger of the two burning buildings. The squeals of terrified animals coiled up with the smoke. Ted dismounted in the open yard between house and barn.

"Anybody there?" he called.

No one answered, but it dawned on him that anyone inside might be afraid he was one of the raiders come back. He charged to the house and ripped open the front door. A wave of heat slammed him in the face. He could feel his skin withering and he backed away. Dropping to the floor, he tried to look in under the heavy cloud of smoke belching from the open door.

He crawled close, poking his head through the doorway. He could still feel searing heat on his head and shoulders, but it wasn't as bad as the first time.

"Anyone there?" he called again.

Again he got no answer, but as he was

about to back away, he heard a thump from somewhere deep inside the boiling cloud. He tried to crawl inside, but the heat was too much for him. The smoke was thickening and slowly lowering toward the floor.

Backing out, he ran around the side of the house, looking for a window. He could see nothing through the first one. At the second, he thought he caught a glimpse of something moving, but he couldn't be sure.

Ted tried to raise the window, but it wouldn't budge. Standing back, he planted a foot on the glass and pushed. The glass cracked, then fell into the house. Another wave of heat spewed out through the broken glass. Ted used the butt of his Colt to knock more glass from the frame, then leaned in. The smoke wasn't as thick here, but it soon would be.

On the floor, partially wreathed in smoke, he saw what might have been a bundle of rags. He stared at it for a moment, uncertain whether he had seen it move. As he was about to pull away from the window, he heard a moan. It might have been the bundle, but he wasn't sure. Ted knocked the rest of the glass loose, then hoisted one leg in through the window. He could feel the heat through his dungarees.

Inside, he dropped to the floor and bunched his handkerchief over his nose and mouth with one hand. Using his free hand to grope ahead of him in the thickening smoke, he felt his fingertips brush the cloth. Stretching out full length on the floor, he was able to grab enough of the cloth to tug on it with his fingers. It resisted, and he pushed deeper into the cloud. This time he was able to close his hand over part of the bundle. It was too heavy for a pile of rags.

Pulling it toward him, he rose to his knees, still covering his nose and mouth. The acrid smoke made his eyes water and he was afraid he'd lost his sense of direction. Jerking the bundle against his knees, he let the handkerchief go and lifted with both hands. Ted staggered toward the window, now just a gray smear in the smoke. The heat swirled around him, and smoke billowed, and he could feel the rush of hot air pass him.

Ted found the window again, but his lungs felt as if they were ready to burst. Leaning against the wall, he dumped the bundle through the opening, then leaned forward. He gulped for air, but there was too much smoke and he fell forward. He was conscious of landing hard, then his head started to swim.

He coughed and his head ached as he tried to crawl away from the burning house. Ted dragged the bundle behind him, but his eyes hurt too much to open, and he still wasn't sure who or what he had dragged from the flames.

Lying on his stomach, he felt his guts heave, and he turned to one side, waiting for his breakfast to spew out. Convulsions racked him, but nothing came up. He gulped air through his mouth, swallowing it like cold water. Every mouthful burned, but he kept on, coughing and hacking to clear his lungs.

He blacked out for a moment, and when he came to, he felt as if he were spinning slowly on some kind of revolving platform. The sky swam across his vision, and the black smoke pulsed toward him, backed away, then came down as if to swallow him again.

His hands hurt, and the skin of his neck and face felt like it had been peeled away with a skinning knife.

Slowly his head started to clear. He became conscious of a low moan somewhere near him. He reached out with a hand, still having difficulty opening his eyes. He found the bundle and realized it was a small person, probably a child. With a roar, the rafters of the barn gave way and the roof collapsed. He turned to look, but saw only a blur. The nearest wall sagged inward, and as Ted watched through watery eyes, it fell, sending a shower of sparks into the air.

He wiped at his eyes with a sleeve. Turning on his stomach, he looked around, hoping to spot a well. He found a horse trough, over near the barn. It was close to the flames, but he thought he could get to it. Staggering toward it, he ripped off his shirt. At the trough, he plunged the shirt into the water and wrapped it around his head. The water was warm, but it soothed his skin. He let the water run down over his chest and shoulders, then scooped a handful to rinse his eyes. He could see a little better now and spotted a pail at one end of the trough.

Scooping a pailful of water, he staggered back to the crumpled bundle. Ted emptied the pail of water, and the ball uncurled. He could see it was a girl about twelve or thirteen years old. She lay on her back now, and Ted knelt beside her.

Mopping at her with the soaking shirt,

he patted her cheeks. "Come on, honey, wake up," he whispered.

The girl moaned, and he patted her cheeks again. She stopped moaning, then darted straight up. The scream cut through him like a razor. It started high and went higher still, in one long, shuddering shriek.

"It's alright, honey, it's alright," he said.

"Papa, where's Papa, where's Papa?" She turned to him, blinking away the water streaming from her hair. "I want my papa." She broke off in a fit of coughing. He thought for a moment she was going to gag, but she fought it off.

She screamed again, then buried her face in her hands.

"What happened, darlin'?"

She shook her head, mumbling something into her hands. Ted didn't catch it, and she wouldn't repeat it when he asked.

"Is your father here somewhere?"

She lowered her hands, tilted her head toward him in spasmodic jerks, like some sort of wading bird. Her eyes were bulging and her mouth moved in silent terror.

"Where's your father?" Ted repeated.

She pointed to the house.

"Your father's in the house?"

She nodded. "In the house."

Ted shook his head. There was no way in

hell he could get back inside. The roof was already sagging on its beams. Smoke poured from every window, leaving thick clots of soot on the outside walls above them. Flames already licked at the window frames from inside.

The girl tried to get up, and Ted reached out to hold her down. She turned to him. "I have to get Papa."

"Honey, you can't go in there."

"I have to."

"It's too late." As if to underline the truth of his words, the roof caved in with a shudder. The girl screamed again, scratching at Ted's hands to get loose. He held on and she stopped struggling. Looking into his face, she seemed to be asking him what had happened.

Ted noticed that one cheek was badly bruised, and a lip had been split. A thin trickle of blood, almost dry, ran from a corner of her mouth and down her chin. She seemed to realize what he was looking at and wiped at her chin with a torn sleeve. The blood came away in flakes.

He realized all her clothing had been torn. Her dress, now soaked from the trough water, had been ripped down the front. She grew conscious of his gaze and tugged the tatters around her. Hugging herself tightly, she started to rock back and forth.

"What happened in there?" Ted asked. "Before the fire?"

She shook her head. "Nothing."

"Don't lie to me," Ted snapped. "Did they hurt you?"

She seemed confused by the question. Staring at him with wide eyes, she shook her head again, this time with less conviction.

"They did, didn't they?"

She looked at the ground.

"It's alright. It wasn't your fault."

"They . . ."

"Never mind, darlin'. It's going to be alright. They'll pay for it, I promise you."

She shook her head again, this time vigorously.

"Does anyone else live here with you?"

"No," she whispered.

"Where's your mother?"

"Dead." She looked at him again. "Like Papa."

Ted stood, then reached down to help her up. She refused at first, cringing away from his hand. He dropped to one knee and put an arm around her shoulders. She tried to shrink away, but he held on, pulling her close. She collapsed suddenly,

throwing herself into his arms and sobbing.

"Come on," he said. "We have to get you somewhere safe."

"There is no safe place. Not here. Not without Papa . . ."

"We'll see about that," Ted said.

17

Ted tried to get the girl to talk to him, but she just ignored him completely. Nothing worked, small talk, stern interrogation, pleading. No matter how he tried to break through to her, she just stared back at him from eyes that seemed to grow deeper by the second as she retreated further and further into herself. She watched the world, but no longer cared to be part of it.

When they reached the mess wagon, he filled Cookie in, and it was the old man who suggested Ted take her to the O'Hara farm. "They got no kids of their own, but it would be best for the girl to have somebody around her. You cain't stay here and watch her all day. She don't want an old geezer like me around here, neither. Maybe Mrs. O'Hara can get her to open up a little."

Rather than ask them, Ted decided to

bring the girl, in a way giving them no choice. They seemed decent enough people, and it was hard to think they might turn her away. At least it was worth a shot. Ted threw a spare saddle on his second horse and boosted her into the saddle. It was a two-hour ride, but there was nothing else he could do, not if he considered the girl's condition and the reality of his own life at the moment.

As they left the wagon behind, Ted chose not to say anything. The girl knew what he was planning, because he knew she heard everything that was said. She was terrified, and he understood that, but she was a liability he couldn't afford.

She frowned at him now and then, but said nothing for the first hour. She watched him from the corner of her eye, never looking directly at him, but never letting him out of her sight for a minute. Once, he heard something off the road ahead and told her to stay put while he checked it out. It was nothing but a stray cow caught in some brambles, but when he rode back to her, the stark terror on her face was unmistakable.

And every time Ted looked at her, his heart broke. Terrible bruises on her cheek and forehead had turned an ugly purplish black. Her hair was matted, and there was no brush to pull the burrs and knots loose. Even five feet away, Ted could smell the fire on her, an acrid stench, ashes and smoke, smelling like death smelled. The way the killing fields of Shiloh smelled.

Ted chewed at his lower lip until it was raw. He kept working his tongue over the skinned flesh, almost enjoying the sting of it. It made him feel alive, at least. And on that one point, he needed constant reassurance.

For the rest of the ride, the kid kept glancing at him, as if she wanted to say something, but didn't know how. Ted waited patiently. He thought about prompting her, giving her an opening, but he didn't know how. Finally, he decided that someone else, someone she didn't associate so directly with the fire and her father's death, would have to make the breakthrough.

When they reached the O'Hara place, the yard was quiet. O'Hara heard their horses and came out of the barn. He had a shotgun with him this time and carried it cradled in his arms. It was obvious he was uncomfortable with the weapon. And equally obvious was the fact that he wouldn't stand a chance against anybody who knew how to use a gun.

He recognized Ted when he got closer, and the anxious frown relaxed a little. He looked at the girl, then at Ted, as if to ask who she was.

"Cotton," he said. "See you're still here."

"That surprise you?" Ted asked.

"I wouldn't be, if I was you."

Ted nodded.

"Come on down." He walked toward the porch and Ted walked his horse to the hitching post, slipped out of the saddle, and helped the girl to the ground. He tied both horses and started onto the porch, but the girl grabbed his arm.

"What's the matter with her? And who is she?" O'Hara asked.

"I don't want to answer the first question right now, and I can't answer the second one."

O'Hara seemed confused for a moment, then shrugged it off. "Come on in." He stepped into the house, then stood in the doorway.

"I'll be along in a minute," Ted told him.

To the girl, he said, "Listen, these are good people. They can help you, if you let them."

She shook her head.

"Look, somebody's got to take care of you. You must have folks somewhere. We have to get in touch with them, and you need to stay someplace while we do."

Again, she shook her head.

Ted was about to shout at her, thinking maybe that would jar her loose from whatever had its claws in her, when Millie O'Hara appeared on the porch.

"Mr. Cotton, what's going on? Why don't you two come on in out of the sun?"

"I was asking her the same thing," Ted said.

Millie stepped off the porch, and her husband started to follow. She heard his boots on the porch and turned to him, shaking her head. "You go on inside, Kevin, I'll take care of it." She stepped between the two horses. One glance told her something terrible had happened to the girl. She shooed Ted away. "Go on inside. Talk about cows, or something," Millie said.

Ted, grateful for the dismissal, stepped away. The girl still grabbed his sleeve, but Millie gently untangled her fingers from the cloth. Even as he backed away, Ted saw the fingers close over Millie's wrist. The skin of the woman's arm turned white on either side of the grip.

O'Hara waited in the doorway, stepped aside for Ted, then gestured toward the table. "Pull up a chair," he said.

When Ted was seated, O'Hara sat opposite him. "What happened?" He asked the question in such a way as to suggest he already knew the answer.

"Conlee killed her father and burned the place to the ground. I think the girl was raped. The bastards left her in the burning house. Nearly got myself barbecued getting her out."

"It might have been better if you left her."

Ted didn't believe what he'd just heard. "Are you crazy, man?"

"What's going to happen to her now?"

"She must have family. We can find them, see that she gets there, wherever that happens to be."

"Cotton, this is a hard country. Hard things happen. It's nobody's fault, it's just the way it is."

"What was I supposed to do? Walk away from it?"

O'Hara shrugged. "I would've. For all you know, Conlee'll come back for her. He doesn't usually leave witnesses."

"No! No way in hell would I leave that girl there. What kind of man are you, O'Hara?"

"A man who understands reality, Cotton." He sighed. "Look, I don't mean to sound harsh, but you've got to face facts, man. You can't go traipsing across Kansas on some sort of fool's errand with that girl trailing behind you. You'll probably get yourself killed anyhow, but even if you don't, you can't have her along."

"I was hoping you and your wife would take her in. Just until we can find her family."

O'Hara shook his head. "Sorry, Cotton. I can't do that."

"Why not?"

"It's a mistake, that's why. I don't need Conlee comin' after me. I'm doin' okay here. That's the way I want to keep it."

"What about tomorrow? What about next week?"

"I'll worry about that later."

"And when Conlee runs out of farms to burn? What then? What happens when it's Millie's turn to provide a little fun for those animals? What do you do then?"

"It won't come to that. I mind my own business. That's how I get along in the world."

"What about the sheriff? Can she at least stay here until I get him to take her?"

"He won't. Tom Mitchell's a practical

man, just like I am. We're on the edge of the knife here, Cotton. If we forget about that for a second, we're finished."

"You're already finished, you ask me, O'Hara. You make me sick."

"Oh, I do, do I? From what I hear, you're no great shakes standing up to Comanches. What makes you think Conlee is any different?"

Ted kicked back his chair and stood up. He was so furious he could merely shake his head. Words escaped him. And deep inside was the hot and heavy truth that O'Hara just might be right. It sat there like a ball of molten lead in his gut. He turned and walked to the door.

"You better think about what I just said," O'Hara called.

Ted pushed open the door and stepped onto the porch. Millie was just coaxing the girl up the steps. The girl was hanging back, and Millie squeezed her arm, just the way the girl had squeezed her own a few minutes before.

"Come on, Margaret. It's okay. Come on with me. You need something to eat. You'll feel better."

"Forget about it, Mrs. O'Hara, she's coming with me."

Millie looked stunned. "What do you

mean? She can't. She needs someone to look after her."

"Your husband won't let her stay."

"He what?"

"He doesn't want her here. Says it's too dangerous. He won't let her stay."

The girl darted up the steps and wrapped her arms around Millie's waist. She buried her face in the woman's skirts and started to sob.

"We'll just see about that, Mr. Cotton," Millie said. "Come with me, child."

She barged through the door, the girl hanging on for dear life, and Ted followed. O'Hara was sitting at the table, his eyes staring off into some unseen distance. He glanced at Millie, but said nothing. Ted noticed that O'Hara's eyes were red-rimmed, and the Irishman must have realized it, because he swiped a big paw over them, then let it land on the table with a thud.

"Mr. Cotton tells me you want to throw this child to the wolves. Is that right?"

O'Hara looked at his wife, but remained silent. "Answer me, Kevin O'Hara. Is that right?"

"What else can we do, Millie? What else can we do?"

"We can stand up for ourselves. We can

say this has gone far enough. We can say no more, dammit. No more!"

"What's come over you, woman?"

"What's come over *me,* is it? You can sit there and ask me that? It's not me wants to throw this poor child away like a piece of trash. Suppose it had been me, and not this girl. What then? Would you throw me out?"

O'Hara stared at her as if she'd lost her mind.

"Answer me, Kevin. Would you? Would you throw *me* out, too?"

"Of course not. You're my wife, Millie. I could never do that."

"Then you'll not do it to her, either. Not as long as I'm living in this house, you won't."

"But . . ."

"No, Kevin. There are no buts. Not this time. I've stood by and watched you, and all the others; the sheriff, Darren McGovern, Jason Hillyer, one by one, you caved in, like tenpins. And now, Ralph Conlee's the only man in this territory who does what he wants to do, because you men don't have the spine to do what you *ought* to do."

"You've no call to talk to me that way, Millie. Not in front of strangers."

"Oh, and who should I talk to that way, if not the man I married? What happened to you, Kevin? You were always a good man. I didn't want the world. I was lucky to have you. That's what I used to think. But now . . ."

She turned to the girl. Stroking her hair, she turned away from the two men. The girl was sobbing quietly, her knuckles white where her fingers dug into the folds of Millie's skirt.

"Don't worry, child, you'll be safe here." Then, turning back to O'Hara, she said, "Won't she, Kevin? Won't she be safe here?"

O'Hara nodded.

"Then tell her, dammit. Tell her she'll be safe here. Tell her Conlee and those animals of his will never lay a finger on her again. Tell her, dammit. Tell her now!"

O'Hara looked at Ted. But Ted was as stunned by the onslaught as O'Hara. He shrugged.

Getting up from his chair, O'Hara walked toward Millie. He put a stiff arm around her, then knelt down beside the girl. "It's alright, honey. Don't you worry. Nobody can hurt you here. Not now."

But his voice shook, and Ted knew the man was trying to convince himself more than the girl.

"Look," Ted said, "I'll have Cookie bring the wagon. He can stay here with you. An extra man won't hurt."

"That's a good idea," Millie said. "Maybe we can convince some of the others, too. Maybe it's time everybody took a good look in the mirror. It would be nice to like what we see, for a change."

18

For nearly a week, Ted crisscrossed the countryside, looking for something, anything, that would lead him to Conlee and his men. There was plenty of evidence that he had passed through, but the trail was always cold. There were rumors, but the Kansas hills seemed to be as fertile soil for them as for any other crop.

Then, on the sixth day after he'd pulled Margaret Reynolds from her burning house, he got lucky. Ted picked up the trail first thing in the morning. Tracking wasn't difficult, because Conlee and his men rode like they had nothing to be afraid of. And from what Ted had seen so far, they were dead right.

The desire for revenge was burning like a hard, bright jewel on the edge of the horizon. What had been purely personal, an eye for an eye, Conlee's life for Johnny's, had become much more. It was still personal, but Ted was starting to look at things in a new way.

He could sense that Jacob would disagree, but Jacob lived in some other world, where men were perfect and the rules worked. The more Ted looked at it, the more clearly he understood that rules existed precisely because men like Ralph Conlee existed. Without them, rules wouldn't be necessary.

But rules on paper were worthless. Worthless, too, was a man with a badge who wouldn't use a gun. It seemed so elementary, and yet it came as a revelation. It seemed almost like Ted was the first man to understand that rules had to be enforced, that blood had to be spilled in defense of those rules, if it were necessary. And it could not have been more necessary than this time. Ralph Conlee had been grinding the law, the good book, and just about anything else anyone held sacred under his heel for so long, it no longer seemed to matter to anyone.

But Ted wasn't going to let it go. He couldn't. Not as long as he could breathe. He didn't owe these people anything. But it went beyond that. He owed Johnny, and he owed Margaret. And, most of all, he owed himself. Life had played a rather cruel joke on him, and he had stood there like a village idiot, second-guessing himself, and wondering why everyone was laughing. He might as well have let the drool run down his chin.

He knew that his worst mistake would be underestimating Conlee. The man might be little better than a monster now, but he had led a brigade of guerrillas for four years. He had stayed alive and, presumably, had kept a few of his men alive as well. Given the meat grinder the War Between the States had been, that was no little accomplishment. It didn't earn Conlee respect, but it sure as hell made him a dangerous man to buck.

Riding after him on a crisp, bright morning, Ted felt like his whole life had somehow been preparation for what was about to begin. It was almost perfect in its biblical simplicity. He was David going after Goliath. But it was easy to identify with a winner. Becoming one yourself was another matter.

Common sense told Ted that Conlee must have some sort of permanent camp within a day or two's ride. Even guerrillas had to sleep someplace.

Past midday, Ted passed the still-smoking ruins of a small homestead. He reined in and walked to the edge of the foundation. The only thing still standing was the stone chimney. It pointed at the sun like an obscene finger. Among the ruins, the remains of someone's life. An old piano, its strings snapped and curling like tormented snakes, sat in what had been one corner of the house. Hunks of metal, tarnished by the heat of the blaze, dotted the heaped ashes. Most were no longer recognizable.

Ted stepped into the wreckage. His boots kicked up clouds of ash. Still glowing coals winked as the air hit them. He could feel the heat through the soles of his boots. Walking over to the corner, he touched several of the piano strings. His fingers came away black. He rubbed the ashes between his fingertips, then licked them clean. The bitter taste made him thirsty and a little angry.

In another corner, a mound of ash caught his eye. He stepped around what must have been a chair, its covering gone, its stuffing charred away to wispy curls of ash, and nudged the mound with his toe. A skin of ash collapsed, like glass breaking without a sound. He turned away from the bones.

He'd seen things like this before, in Texas. The Comanches made torching an art. But that was different. That was, after all, war of a sort. This was something else again. This was plain evil, the kind of evil Jacob and Ellie Quitman didn't want to admit existed.

Ted backed away from the bones, nearly tripping over something hidden in the cinders. He bumped something with his shoulder, a pipe of some sort, maybe a clothes rack, and it teetered. He spun around, reaching for it with both hands, lost control, and it tipped back and past him. It cracked against something that sounded like stone. Ted didn't want to turn around, but he knew he had to.

Stripped of its covering of ash, the skull stared at him with that final, permanent grin.

Stepping over the rock foundation, he looked beyond the ruined house, past the chimney. A fenced-in garden, mostly vegetables, but sporting a few flowers, looked desperate against the afternoon sky. Ted walked to the fence and leaned over to snatch at a flower. It came away reluctantly, and then only after he pinched the stem between thumb and fingernails. Holding the flower in his hand for a moment, he wondered who had planted it. He knew only too well that someone who had cared for the garden now lay there in the ashes. As he walked back past the ruined house, he stopped for a moment and set the flower on its stem on the foundation. He thought of Ellie, and for a second was tempted to say a prayer.

But the temptation passed. Praying was now for other people.

Remounting, Ted pushed on past the ruined homestead. The road was pocked with prints from recent, heavy traffic. He had seen more than a dozen men the day before, but there could have been more. To keep himself from worrying about what he would do once he found Conlee's camp, he concentrated on the search.

Another hour's hard riding brought him within sight of several columns of smoke. They were three or four miles ahead, and almost certainly marked some sort of camp. Ted cut off the road and into the open plains. If the war had taught him anything, it was that risk was unavoidable, but only a fool took risks he didn't have to.

Angling to the north, he made a broad circle. It took him more than an hour, and when he finally had the sun at his back, he dismounted at a grove of cottonwoods.

Tugging his pony deep into the trees, he hobbled it securely and jerked his Winchester carbine from the saddle boot. Filling his shirt pocket with extra shells, he started back toward the columns of smoke on foot. After a half hour, he was sweating and winded. The land wasn't as flat as it looked, instead being an unbroken succession of gentle hills and shallow valleys. It wasn't as bad as the rocky waste of the Llano Estacado, the barren high desert of the western panhandle, but the going was tough enough.

Mounting the last ridge but one between him and the smoke, Ted lay flat when he got within a few yards of the top. He knew he wouldn't be able to see the camp itself, but Conlee was almost certain to have sentries posted on high ground. He wished he'd brought his father's old mariner's telescope, but the naked eye would have to do.

Wriggling like a worm up the last few yards to the hilltop, he took off his hat and pressed himself as flat as possible. Just his brow and a thatch of sandy hair poked above the ridge. With the sun at his back, he had a little extra advantage. The sentries would have to squint to see him at all, and to be certain, they'd need binoculars or a telescope.

For several minutes, the ridge across the last valley looked deserted. He found it hard to believe that Conlee could have been that cocky. There *had* to be lookouts somewhere on the next ridge. Starting at the left, Ted scanned the ridge line yard by yard without any luck. It was too good to be true. He was tempted to cross the valley and see if he could get a look at the camp from the next ridge. Giving it another minute, he held his breath, trying to avoid the least movement that might disrupt his scrutiny.

Just as he was about to stand up, a distant drumbeat, hooves on sod, echoed across the valley. Almost instinctively, he flattened himself deeper into the shallow grass, until he felt like a ribbon with eyes. A moment later, three horsemen broke the ridge line. They reined in, and one dismounted. Ted watched as the three men discussed something, then the two still on horseback turned and disappeared back behind the ridge. The third man dropped to his haunches and balanced a carbine across bony knees.

Ted let his breath out slowly, as if afraid the sentry might be able to hear normal breathing. He was looking so hard at the guard, it seemed as if the man was just an arm's length away. But he was almost faceless in the glare. The bright sun reflected off his skin, washing out shadow and contour. The only thing Ted was sure of was the thick, black mustache drooping on either side of a scraggly beard clinging desperately to a craggy jaw.

The man wore a blue jacket that looked like it had been repaired more than once. Remnants of yellow ribbon still clung to the shoulders, and epaulettes, blackened almost as dark as the blue of the coat's cloth, jiggled when the sentry moved. Knee-high boots were the only other detail Ted could discern. If this man wasn't one of Conlee's raiders, he should have been.

There was nothing he could do now until nightfall.

Ted retreated back down the slope until it was safe to stand. He trudged back to the cottonwoods and took some dried beef from a saddlebag. Washing it down with water, he sat down with his back against a tree to wait for dark. Overhead, birds, getting used to his presence, began to chirp. Out of the sun, a slight breeze wafting through the trees, it seemed almost idyllic. Only the weight of the shells in his pocket wouldn't let him forget why he was sitting there.

The sun took forever to run out of steam. Ted shifted restlessly, watching the pattern of shade twist and turn in the breeze. Gradually, the shadows thickened, and the sky darkened like an aging bruise. The shadows began to lose their definition, and finally it was dark.

Ted took a long, deep breath, then hauled himself to his feet. He grabbed the Winchester leaning against the tree and climbed into the saddle. This time, he would ride to the foot of the last hill. If they got wind of him, he would be dead without the pony. He took the approach at an easy pace, not wanting the hooves to give him away. Even the creak of saddle leather made him nervous.

The man on the hill, or whoever had replaced him, would have a keen ear for anything out of the ordinary. It was how he stayed alive. There was no moon, and the sky was a blue so deep it was almost black. Still, flickering along with the stars, thin strands of whitish gray smoke, thin as ropes, coiled up into the night.

A faint glow from a half-dozen fires smeared the air with a hint of orange. Against the dim light, the smoke looked thicker and darker. Ted dismounted and started up the hill, quietly levering a shell into the Winchester's chamber. He muffled the click as best he could with his free palm. As the lever clicked back into place, it felt like the final piece of a jigsaw puzzle slipping home, locking the whole fragile construction into some stable figure. It wouldn't stand up to much, but at least it was complete.

Drifting to the left as he neared the crest, he tried to pick out the sentry on the far hill, but it was impossible to see any details at all. He curved to the left, coming at the hill end on as he dropped into the valley. If he couldn't see someone he knew was there, he at least had a slim chance that the sentry couldn't see him, either.

He climbed toward the orange glow, angling for a shallow notch. Dropping to his belly, he crawled up the very center of the vee until he could look down into the next valley. Somewhere above and to his right, the sentry sat oblivious. And below him, he saw the camp. Six fires and, at first blush, at least thirty bedrolls, possibly more. Conlee had a small army.

And Ted Cotton was alone.

19

Ted crept closer, listening to the scattered noise from the camp below. From the sound of it, several of the men were drinking heavily. At one point, he froze when a gunshot cracked. He thought he had been spotted, but instead of a headlong charge up the hillside, the men rushed toward one of the fires.

Two men squared off close to the flames, the others gathered around as the center men circled each other. The fight erupted all of a sudden when one of the men charged the other. Both fell to the ground, and the others closed in for a few seconds, egging the combatants on.

The circle expanded again as both men struggled to their feet. Even at this distance, Ted could hear the grunts of the men as they swung and missed. Now and then a punch would connect, and the thud of fist on flesh sounded like a poleax felling a steer for slaughter.

All of the men, audience and fighters, were etched like charcoal smears. Their shadows twisted like panic-stricken snakes as the circle opened and closed. The two men at the center occasionally passed close to the flames. Three men threw a few more logs on the fire. As the blaze grew brighter, smearing the men with red light, faces appeared in the darkness whenever the men would fall and the ring would tighten. Then, when they'd regained their feet and the audience backed away, it looked like a circle of headless men.

The fight was heating up now. One of the boxers, a small, wiry man with a beard, tripped his opponent. The other man fell heavily, and the little guy was on him in a flash. Straddling the bigger man's chest, he locked his hands around the man's throat. Rocking forward to increase the pressure, he threw his whole body into the stranglehold.

The man on the bottom flailed helplessly, his fists waving in the air as he tried to slug his strangler. As the pressure increased, he grabbed hold of both wrists and tried to rip away the hands. He was starting to lose consciousness when a huge man in a Federal blue jacket suddenly stepped into the center of the ring.

The bearded giant grabbed the wiry man by both shoulders and lifted him to his feet. "That's enough," the giant shouted. "Let him up, Billy."

But Billy wouldn't let go. As the giant lifted him, he clung to his opponent's throat, hauling the larger man with him as the giant tugged. With a vicious kick, the big man broke the stranglehold, snapping his boot across both wrists, then kicking the other man in the chest, the way a lumberjack might kick a log free of his ax.

Tossing the wiry guy aside, he reached down and hauled the nearly unconscious man to his feet. He shook the man by his shirtfront. "Dumb bastards, all of you. What the hell is going on here?"

The giant looked around the circle, which grew larger as he turned to stare at the men, one by one. Soon, the ranks broke, and the men started to skulk away.

But the little guy wasn't finished. He brushed past the giant and barreled into his groggy opponent, knocking him to the ground again. Again, he locked his hands around the man's throat. This time, the giant didn't try to pull him off. He stood there, watching, while the strangled man's feet started to kick, his heels drumming on the ground. Even from the hilltop, Ted could hear the thuds. Then the feet were still. The wiry guy gave one more squeeze for good measure, then started to get to his feet.

The giant moved in. It happened so fast, Ted didn't realize what he was doing until the big man backed away. In his hand, a skinning knife caught the flames for a few seconds, flashing like some sort of magic sword. In the firelight, the blade was almost black along one edge, and it took Ted a moment to realize it was blood.

The wiry man grabbed his own throat, turning toward the giant and grappling at his neck. It looked as if he were trying to strangle himself, now that his opponent was dead.

The giant had cut his throat.

The little man staggered a few steps, then lost his balance and toppled into the flames. The clothing caught fire and the giant laughed.

"Throw a few more logs on the barbecue," he shouted.

The little man thrashed in the flames sending a column of sparks up into the night, then he, too, lay still. Ted could smell the burning flesh as the wind carried past the fire and up the hillside. He wanted to gag, but couldn't.

The big, bearded man, who could only be Ralph Conlee, drew a gun and fired it into the air. "Get back here, all of you," he shouted.

Ted lay there gasping for air. It was as if someone had kicked him in the stomach and emptied his lungs. Every breath hurt, and he was sure he would never breathe normally again.

A few of the men reappeared within reach of the firelight. One of them bent to grab a boot to haul the dead man from the fire, but the big man kicked at him. "Let the bastard burn. I told him to stop. He didn't. You all know what that means, don't you?"

When no one answered him, he said, "You all make me sick. Lazy cowards. Dumb bastards, all of you. I ought to cut all your throats. Who's next?"

There were no takers.

"Like I keep tellin' you," he shouted, tilting his head back and bellowing up into the night sky, "there's room for only one chief. Everybody else is an Indian. Discipline, discipline, discipline. That's what command is all about. And I'm in command. Unless anybody has any other ideas."

He scanned the ring of men, most of whom were keeping well back out of his reach. There was a silence so perfect it was broken only by the crackle of flames and the explosion of a single knot, which sent a shower of sparks up through the column of smoke.

Conlee laughed again, wiped the blade on his pants, and tucked it out of sight. He stepped away from the fire and disappeared. Then his voice drifted through the darkness, "I'm goin' for a ride. Anybody wants to come, saddle up."

Ted, still struggling to breathe, watched as several shadows flitted past the campfires. Ten minutes later, he saw the first of the horsemen drift past the largest fire, wheel his horse and sit there, looking back at the camp. A moment later, another joined him, then a third. Ted couldn't wait. There was nothing he could do with the whole camp, but Conlee was going to expose himself a little. Ted backed down the hill until he found his horse.

He tugged the pony back up the hillside, this time forced to ignore the possibility of the sentry. He hoped the lookout had been drawn down to the camp by the fight, or at least would have relaxed his vigilance a bit. But if he stayed down below, Ted might not be able to fall in behind Conlee and his men.

Several gunshots cracked as the horsemen, now nearly a dozen, galloped back and forth, jumping over the fires and sending their mates scattering for cover. Conlee appeared at last. Brandishing a sword, he charged across the camp and off into the darkness. The raiders followed, firing their weapons until they were empty.

Ted jumped into the saddle and swung off to the left, trying to keep within earshot without exposing himself to the campsite. Once the darkness closed over him, he kicked the pony hard and narrowed the gap a bit. The horsemen cut for the road, and Ted fell in behind them. Even over the sound of his own pony, he could hear the thundering hooves of the men ahead of him.

For the time being, he felt safe in charging headlong. Most of the men were drunk, and probably so full of themselves as well that they would pay no attention to security. If he was going to get close, now was the time. He wished for moonlight, but there was nothing to be done about it.

The firing resumed, briefly, then stopped almost as quickly as it had begun. Conlee must have put a stop to it, which meant that he, at least, was still thinking.

They seemed to be riding with a purpose, as if Conlee had a specific destination in mind. He was close enough now that he could see occasional shadows on the road ahead of him, the horsemen outlined against the lighter color of the late summer grass.

As they rode on by the ruined house where Ted had rescued the girl, it dawned on him that they were heading toward the O'Hara farm. It could just be coincidence, but he felt his gut tighten. Conlee couldn't have known he'd taken the girl there. Or could he?

The road, little more than a pair of ruts carved by wagon wheels through the dry grass, veered to the right and broke up over a hill. Ted knew the road forked in the next valley. He slowed as he neared the top.

The raiders were out of sight, already having crested the ridge, and Ted crossed his fingers. He felt guilty about it, as if wishing them away from the O'Hara place was condemning someone else just as innocent. He sat just below the ridge to give the horsemen time enough to reach the fork.

When he could stand the tension no

longer, he urged his pony up and over the top. The riders were bearing down on the fork. Conlee was in the lead, and Ted knew that whichever way he went, the others would follow. There was no way in hell any of them would cross the big man after the demonstration they had all witnessed.

Ted sighed audibly when Conlee took the right branch, carrying him away from the O'Hara place.

The hoofbeats were distant now, and Ted had to push his horse to regain lost ground. His breathing was shallow and his throat was dry. He licked his lips with a pasty tongue. In the back of his mind was the nagging accusation that, now that he had found Conlee, he didn't know what to do. He didn't want to believe it, but it was true, and he knew it.

The riders were no longer in sight when he reached another fork in the road. He slowed to listen, but could no longer hear them. He dropped from the saddle and checked the road. The soil was dry, but recent use would have kicked up some clots of earth that should still be damp.

The left branch of the fork was bone dry. Its soil had been undisturbed for several hours, at least. He let go of the reins and walked a few yards over to the right branch. There he saw the clots of dirt kicked loose by four dozen hooves. Even in the dry ground, there was no mistaking recent traffic.

Ted sprinted back to his horse and vaulted into the saddle. Jerking the reins, he spurred the pony along the right branch. He broke into a full gallop desperate to make up lost time. At the back of his mind was the possibility that this might be his one and only chance to get at Conlee without the full complement of guerrillas around him.

And if he did find them, he still didn't know what he would do.

20

The mounted men pulled up in front of the dark house. Ted crept as close as he dared on horseback. There was practically no cover between him and the house, and he dismounted, tugging his horse into the trees and looping the reins around a low-hanging branch. Ted wormed his way even closer, crawling through knee-high grass. It whispered as it scraped against his clothing, but there was no way to avoid the sound.

The drunken mob a hundred yards away was unlikely to be listening for the sound of one man slipping through grass like a snake on its belly. A light went on in the farmhouse window, and someone shouted from inside.

The window was closed, and Ted was too far away to hear what was said. Most of the raiders were still mounted, but two had dropped to the ground, handing the reins of their mounts to companions. Because he was so much larger than the others, Conlee could still be seen on his horse. One of the men on foot stomped onto the porch and rapped a heavy fist against the door.

"Come on out, we need some help with our winter wheat," someone shouted, and the men laughed.

The man on the porch pounded harder on the front door, and the light inside went out. "Come on out here, you bastard," he shouted. He rapped the door even harder, until its hinges rattled. Another of the men dismounted and moved around the side of the house, where he found a window. Rapping on the window frame, he called to whoever was inside to open up.

When he got no answer, he stepped back a little and kicked at the window frame. He missed, and the glass shattered as the misplaced foot crashed through it. The man lost his balance and fell backward, one leg still sticking through the broken window. He screamed and his companions laughed.

"What's the matter, Roy? You drunk or somethin'."

Roy jerked his leg back, but it wouldn't move. He screamed again and tried to get up, then lost his balance and lay there moaning.

"Gimme a hand, you sonsabitches. I'm caught." His voice sounded strangely thin. There was a whimper at its edge, all the bravado gone now.

Ted squirmed a few yards closer, trying to get an angle on the side of the house. He could see Roy, one leg still elevated, until two men dismounted and walked over to see what was wrong with him.

"Christ, Roy," one of them said. "You're bleeding like a damn pig. For chrissakes . . ."

Roy stuck a hand up, and the man who'd spoken grabbed it, helping the injured man to his feet.

Conlee jerked the reins of his horse and spun around the corner of the house. The man at the front door was still alternating between pounding and shouting. As Ted drew another ten yards closer, the man switched from pounding to kicking.

Roy's rescuers lifted him and pulled him away from the window. The movement brought a cry of agony from the injured man, and Conlee sat on his horse, watching.

"Stupid bastard," he shouted. "Roy, you're too damn dumb to live."

Roy continued to moan.

"Christ, there's a piece of glass in his leg,

must be eight inches long."

"Get him up, see if he can walk," Conlee said.

They hauled Roy to his feet, but the injured leg collapsed under him.

The two men lowered Roy to the ground again. One of them leaned close to get a better look. "There's so damn much blood, I can't see nothing."

A brief flicker of a match being lit threw shadows on the side of the house, but the match guttered out almost at once. Conlee dismounted and walked toward the prostrate form as another match flickered. This time, a handful of dry grass was set on fire, for a torch, and the kneeling man leaned over Roy.

"Damn, the whole back of his leg's laid open. He needs a doctor."

"No doctor," Conlee said. "Ain't wastin' time takin' no damn fool to no doctor."

"He'll get gangrene, Major."

"His own damn fault."

Conlee bent to have a look. The motion saved his life. A sharp crack sounded from somewhere inside the house. The rest of the window glass showered over the small knot of men.

"Sonofabitch," Conlee shouted. "Sonofabitch tried to kill me. Come on out of there, you bastard." He shook a fist at the ruined window. Another blast from a shotgun ripped at the frame, scattering buckshot in a three-foot circle as it blew through the remnants of the glass.

"Give me the damn torch," Conlee shouted. "Give it to me," and he snatched at the clump of grass, now burnt most of the way down. He threw it through the open window frame. Another shot answered, and Conlee ducked to one side.

"Check the barn, boys," Conlee shouted, backing away from the window. Roy continued to moan. "Shut up, dammit," Conlee screamed. "Shut the hell up."

"He needs a doc, Major."

Conlee pulled a revolver from his belt and cocked it. Roy moaned again, and Conlee fired twice. Ted saw the wounded man jerk, and his own body nearly bounced with the suddenness of the gunshots.

"He don't need no doc no more," Conlee said. He laughed, and one or two of the men on horseback joined him. "Alright, break in the door, some of you birds. The rest of you see what you can find in the barn. Get some coal oil, too, if you can find any."

The man at the front of the house kicked

more viciously at the door, until it fell in with a squeal of screws pulling loose. The crash of the door on the floor sounded like a clap of thunder.

Another blast from the shotgun ripped through the open doorway, tearing into the man who'd kicked it in. The man flew backward and landed on his back in the dirt.

Conlee laughed again, shaking his head as if he just couldn't understand such stupidity. "How many times I told you, you kick a door in, stay the fuck out of the line of fire?"

The rest of the men swarmed around the house, some racing toward the barn, others looking for windows around the back.

Ted raised his Winchester, trying to get Conlee in his sights, but the big man kept moving like a caged tiger, stalking around the corner of the house and back. The men around him saved his life at least twice, stepping into the line of fire as Ted was about to pull the trigger.

Then he was gone. He sent two men through the doorway and charged in after them. A brilliant light, gone almost as soon as it appeared, flashed in the house. It signaled another blast cracking from the shotgun, this one muffled by something.

A moment later, the brittle cracking of a burst of gunfire from inside the house snapped across the grass like a string of firecrackers. In the aftermath, a woman screamed. Conlee reappeared in the doorway, then stepped onto the porch, dragging a woman by one arm.

The men outside cheered, and Conlee bowed. "Told you boys I felt like havin' some fun, didn't I?"

"You can't do no better'n that?" one of the men asked.

Another one of the raiders laughed. "What do you want, Lily Langtry, for chrissakes? You got to take what you can get. This one'll do fine fer now."

The man stepped forward as Conlee let go of the woman's arm. She lay on the ground, curled into a ball. Conlee prodded her with a foot, and she screamed again. Conlee waved in disgust, then stepped back away from the woman. The other man, a string bean with a mop of hair that made him look like a used broom, bent down and grabbed the woman by the hair. She tried to fight him off and dug her nails into the man's wrist. He cursed and slapped at her twice, then grabbed hold of her nightdress and ripped it open.

Ted licked his lips, bringing the Winchester around and waiting for Conlee to stand still long enough to draw a steady bead. But long years of warfare had done their work. Conlee paced constantly, the way officers on the front lines had always done, to keep the enemy sharpshooters off balance. A stationary officer was a dead officer.

Conlee was no officer, but he thought like one, and he had more power and more inclination to abuse it than anyone Ted had ever seen. The string bean opened his fly and dropped onto the woman with a grunt as she scissored her legs and kicked at him.

Two more raiders walked over, as casual as if they were standing in line to buy a newspaper, and reached down to take an ankle each. They pulled the woman's legs apart, and the string bean grinned at one of them over his shoulder. The woman had stopped screaming, knowing it would do her no good.

And Ted couldn't take it anymore. If he couldn't get a shot at Conlee, he could nail the string bean. He sighted on the man about shoulder high. The attacker was propped on his hands, as if doing pushups. It was close, but Ted wondered whether it was better to lie there and do nothing or take the chance of hitting the woman by accident. He thought for a moment of Ellie, and how he would feel if she were the one being raped, and he knew he was going to shoot the bastard even before the answer formed in his mind.

He bit down on his tongue, then squeezed the trigger. The shot exploded like a stick of dynamite. Ted heard the sound of it echo off the walls of the barn. The raiders heard it too, and all but Conlee looked around to see where it had come from. Conlee was the only one with enough presence of mind to dive for cover.

Ted heard the woman scream again, and he glanced just long enough to see her scrambling out from underneath the body of her rapist. She ran toward the house, then seemed to change her mind and veered off into the darkness. One of the raiders sprinted after her, and Ted fired again.

He saw the raider fall, then turned and crawled for all he was worth through the grass. He reached the tree line as shouts echoed behind him. He heard footsteps as several of the raiders charged through the grass. Ted turned once and fired quickly, without aiming. He didn't give a damn whether he hit anyone, as long as he slowed them down. He reached the tree line and raced for his horse.

The shouts drew closer, and he kicked his horse once as he jerked the reins to wheel toward the far side of the trees. He heard hoofbeats as several of the raiders charged across the open field on horseback. He wondered whether he had let his temper get the best of him. But he didn't wonder long. He knew what the woman would say, and that was good enough.

Scattered gunfire cracked behind him, but he knew it was more to terrorize him than to hit him. No way they could see him, he thought. Not yet. The raiders split into two packs. He heard a half-dozen horses wheel to the right in an effort to skirt the trees and catch him as he broke through. At least one broke to the left, and he wondered whether it might be Conlee himself.

Whether it was Conlee or not, the odds were better to the left, and Ted broke for a gap in the trees dead ahead. His pony spurted through the opening and out into the grass. The rider to the left hadn't turned the corner yet and Ted jerked the reins to head straight for the endmost tree. He held the Winchester in one hand as he charged headlong for the corner.

A solitary rider loomed up and Ted fired without waiting to see whether it was the guerrilla chief. The shot went wide, but it spooked the rider, who sawed on the reins and tried to swerve to the right. He skirted close to the trees, just missing the last one in line, and the man's horse bucked. The rider was skillful, and he steadied his mount as Ted plunged on toward him.

Using the weight of the barrel to reload the chamber, Ted pivoted the carbine with a flick of his wrist. His finger found the trigger almost immediately and he fired again, this time not twenty yards from the rider, still struggling to control his mount. This time, the bullet found its mark. He heard the man groan, and as he dashed past, the wounded guerrilla fell heavily from his horse.

Ted fired once more as shouts broke out behind him. He charged back toward the house. Only three raiders were still there, busily torching the barn. Ted charged past, this time with the Colt, and emptied the revolver into the scattering knot of arsonists. The house was already fully ablaze, and it would be suicide to stop.

Ted galloped between house and barn and off into the open field. He slowed a bit once he was out of pistol range. He thought about looking for the woman, but he had to push the thought aside. He'd done what he could. The rest was up to her.

He broke across the open field, weaving from left to right and back, on the off chance he might stop a wild shot. He wished he were in Texas, where the terrain would have given him some cover. Here, other than the slight ups and downs of the gentle hills, cover couldn't be had. That made it a flat-out race. Ted liked his pony, but there were limits on what he could, or would, ask the animal to do.

His only hope was that Conlee's men, used to getting what they wanted when they wanted, might tire of the chase. But Conlee was supposed to be a man who hated, above all else, to be challenged on what he believed to be his own ground.

Ted had dared to challenge him.

What price would he have to pay?

21

Ted thundered down the long ridge, keeping just below the crest as he angled across. He had a big enough lead that he just might be able to double back on them. But he had to reach a gap in the hills before Conlee's men made the top of the rise. By cutting the angle, he hoped to pick up a hundred or two hundred yards. It would be close, but it might work.

He lashed at the cow pony with the reins. Glancing back every twenty yards, he strained to see through the Kansas night. The steady rhythm of his horse seemed almost too good to be true. The raiders were riding much larger horses, more like cavalry chargers. They had longer strides, and probably greater speed, over the short haul, but the cow ponies were bred for endurance and maneuverability. If he could keep enough distance between them to keep from getting a bullet in the back, Ted knew he could eventually outrun them.

But it was a large if, and the odds were long. And he was only too aware that Conlee and his men knew the terrain. He was just passing through. As a stranger, he might run in circles, for all he would know. That meant he had to keep the guerrillas in sight long enough to be certain they hadn't outflanked him somehow.

For a brief moment, he thought about running straight for the O'Hara ranch, but he knew it was too close. If he led Conlee and his men there, the momentary relief of having two extra guns on his side might save his skin, but it would doom the O'Haras. Sooner or later, unless Ted killed him first, the O'Haras would be made to pay. And Ted had just gotten a firsthand look at the brutal coin of Conlee's realm. There was no way in hell he would subject Millie to the risk of that kind of savagery.

Ted dipped lower on the slope. He could sense the ground beginning to flatten, but he couldn't see well enough in the dark to know whether he was getting close enough to a break between hills to cut through and reverse his course. So far, there was no sign of the guerrillas on the long ridge. He was tempted to rein in, to listen. But if they were on his tail, the delay might cost him every yard he'd already gained. He couldn't recover quickly enough to make it up again. It was just too much to ask the pony to do.

Swinging slowly right, still on the flat bottomland, he narrowly missed a shallow brook, the pony leaping at the last second. The sudden jump almost threw him, and he had to lean forward to hang on. He cut along the stream on the far side, and it led him through a narrow cut between two hills. A stand of trees suddenly materialized, as if it had grown in seconds, and he skirted it closely, then wheeled the pony in a tight turn.

Ted dropped from the saddle and ran into the trees, pulling the horse after him. He heard hoofbeats approaching as he ducked into the small clump of trees already beginning to lose their leaves. The horse tried to back away, and Ted nearly lost his grip. The thunder of the hooves grew louder as he ducked down behind a small clump of brush.

It sounded as if the raiders were going to ride right over him. They roared past within yards of the trees, and he held his breath, waiting for the inevitable shout. But it didn't come. The thunder slowly faded, dying away like a flash flood in a dry gully.

Then it was gone.

Ted let his breath out slowly, then sank to the ground. His hands trembled, and his lower lip shook uncontrollably with every inhale. He flattened one palm over his chest to hold his bones in place. It felt as if they were trying to pound their way through his skin. His heart beat in his ears for a few moments, then that thunder, too, faded away.

He got to his feet, still shaking, and his legs threatened to give way as he tried to get a boot into the stirrup. It was closer than he thought, closer than he wanted. And he didn't know where the hell to go.

He could ride the flat hills all night, but then what? Where would he go? What could he possibly do? Conlee had nearly three dozen men. Even if he allowed for the man Conlee stabbed at the camp, and the hapless Roy, the numbers were overwhelming. Throw in the three men he'd shot, two of whom were probably dead, the other possibly, and he still had more than thirty. He couldn't do it, and he knew it.

The only way for him to win was to get to Conlee. He knew that if he could somehow sever the head, the body would die. Half of the guerrillas were bound to Conlee by fear, the other half because they looked up to him. Deny them that, take away the fear, and they had no reason to stay.

Or did they?

But he'd never live long enough to find out, if he tried to pare them down a man or two at a time. This nightmare of an army was not a stick he could whittle away a curl at a time. They hadn't yet made the knife that could do that. You took an ax, and you chopped it quickly, cleanly, and unmercifully. Or you walked away and forgot about it. There was no middle ground.

Ted glanced at the stars to get his bearings. It was well after midnight, and he was exhausted. He felt as if he were getting close, but he couldn't do it without sleep. And he needed to talk it through. He needed Cookie, someone he could bounce things off until he could sort out the pieces. A mistake now would be costly, maybe even fatal. But there was just so much time. He felt as if a huge, invisible clock ticked off the seconds, and that some deadline drew closer and closer. He didn't know how much time he had, he knew only that it wasn't enough.

Goading the pony with his spurs, he rode back along the shallow creek, letting the raiders chase their own shadows. For the moment, every stride of their horses took them farther and farther astray. He wished it also bought him time, but that was too much to ask of fate.

He rode like a man half asleep, letting the pony have its head. Every so often, he had to make a choice, and he chose cautiously, staying as far away from the camp as he could, making a broad circle back toward the O'Hara farm.

It was nearly sunup when he broke over the last rise. The first red lip of the sun curled in an inverted sneer over the horizon, flooding the endless sea of grass with scarlet. It grew brighter, and the color leached away as the sun rose. And it seemed to shrink, as if it were contracting into itself, curling into a tighter ball like an armadillo to protect itself from something Ted neither saw nor sensed.

The farm spread out below him, like a postcard he'd seen once in a New Orleans store. Then that unreality faded, too, and the grass turned pale green as the sun came the rest of the way up. He rode down the last hill slowly, trying to fit the scattered pieces of the night together in some way that made sense. He had seen the brutality of Ralph Conlee firsthand. It did nothing to reassure him. The man seemed to have no weakness, because he seemed to have no heart and no soul.

Ted kept thinking of Jacob Quitman, and wondering what the old man would say if he had witnessed the things that Ted had seen that night. He found it hard to believe that Jacob would not be the first man in line to spit on Conlee's corpse.

Or would he?

Maybe that was what made Jacob so special. Maybe the ability to look beyond the gore and the rendered flesh was what gave Jacob his faith. But Ted couldn't look that far. There was too much blood for that, and too much flesh ripped bleeding from the bone. No man should have to forgive that kind of savagery, he thought.

"I sure as hell don't," he whispered as he turned into the narrow, tree-lined lane leading to Kevin O'Hara's farm.

Cookie was up already. The old man sat by the fire, a pot of coffee just beginning to burble. He watched Ted quietly, waiting for him to dismount before getting to his feet.

"Thought you might not be coming back, Teddy."

"What the hell do you mean by that?"
"What do you think I mean?"
"You like the rest of them, Cookie? You lost your faith in me, too?"
"That's not what I meant, and you damn well know it. I was afraid maybe you bit off a mite too much to swallow. A meal like that has a way of turnin' on a feller, can bite him back if he don't look out."
"You're right about that. Conlee would chew me up and spit me out, if I give him the chance."
"How you intend to avoid it?"
"I don't know. I wish to hell I . . ."
A screen door banged, and he turned toward the house without finishing his thought. Millie O'Hara stood on the porch, drying her hands on her apron. She saw him and waved. He waved back, and she stepped off the porch. "You want some breakfast?" she called.
Ted shook his head. "No thanks, ma'am."
She walked toward the wagon, and Ted watched her closely. She was really quite pretty, but did nothing to flaunt it. She dressed simply and took no pains to color her face. A thin white ribbon holding her hair in place was the only concession to vanity.

When she was close enough, she stuck out a hand, and Ted grasped it. Her grip was firm, the hand strong without being aggressive. Then he realized it was how the woman herself had to be, in order to survive out here.

"You look like you had a long night," she said. Her smile was warm, but muted. He nodded, trying to return it, but what he'd been through stole it from his lips before it had fully formed.

"Yeah," he said.

"Want to talk about it?"

"Nope."

"That bad, huh?"

"Worse," Ted said. He thought about asking Millie if she knew the farm Conlee had razed, but that inevitably would lead her to ask questions, questions he didn't want to answer, especially not for a woman.

"Margaret was asking for you."

"How is she?"

"Still terrified. She's talked a little, but not much. She hasn't really told me what happened, but I can guess. The poor child, it must have been hell for her."

"Yeah, well . . ." He stopped because he didn't really know what to say. He looked at her a long moment, then turned to look at the sun. Without turning back to her, he asked, "Is Kevin up?"

"Just finishing breakfast. You can come in for coffee, if you like."

"No thanks. I guess I'll just try some of Cookie's java. It's an acquired taste, but it kind of ruins you for anything else."

"I'm sure it's not that bad."

She smiled, and Ted shook his head. "I'd be lyin' if I agreed with that, Mrs. O'Hara."

"Well, if you change your mind . . ."

"Thank you, but I think I'll just get a little sleep."

"You're welcome to use the guest room. Margaret's up, and she'll be helping me put up some preserves this morning."

"That's alright. I been on the trail long enough, a nice rock is about all the comfort I need. Long as it's the right size."

"You're really not the ruffian you pretend, Mr. Cotton. Don't think I don't know that."

"Yes, ma'am."

She turned to walk back to the house, and Ted watched her quietly.

"That's a married woman, there, Teddy. Don't you be lookin' at her that way. I'll have to tell Ellie Quitman about it."

"Cookie, you old sonofabitch, just pour

me some of that coffee, will you. After I get a nap, we have to have a long talk."

"What about, son?"

Ted didn't answer. There was no need.

22

Kevin O'Hara pounded the table with a huge fist. "Jesus Christ, man," he exploded, "what in the sweet name of Jesus were you thinkin'?"

"I didn't have time to think, Kevin. I did what I had to do. There was no other way."

"You bloomin' idjit. You know what you've done, don't you?"

"Why don't you tell me," Ted said. "I'd love to hear how you would have handled it, too, while you're at it."

"Handled it? Is that what you did? You handled it? Oh, it's a fine mess you've caused us all, Cotton. A fine mess."

Ted watched the big farmer pace back and forth behind the table. He wanted to explain to O'Hara how badly he misunderstood Ralph Conlee, but he knew O'Hara wouldn't listen. He wouldn't listen because he didn't want to hear. He was too damned scared. He knew he was scared, and he'd been scared so damned long he didn't know how not to be.

Finally, O'Hara sighed and sat back down. "You don't know what a hole you've dug, Cotton. Deep enough to bury us all, it is. And that's a plain fact."

Millie O'Hara sat silently through it all. She watched each man in turn during the exchange. Ted was conscious of her gaze and sensed that she wanted to speak. But there was no opening for her, none long enough for her to overcome her hesitancy.

"Kevin, I know what you think, but I'm telling you, that woman was as good as dead unless I shot that bastard. How would you have handled it? Would you have turned and ridden away? Do you really think that's an answer?"

"It's not an answer, no. But there doesn't have to be one. There's no damned question. We *know* what Conlee is like. We don't have to consider possibilities. There *are* none."

"You can't turn your back on something like that, Kevin. I know I can't anyway."

"That's because it's personal for you. You have a score to settle, man. Good God, can't you see that? It makes a difference. It makes all the difference in the world."

"And you don't have a score to settle, is that it? That woman's husband doesn't matter to you. He was a neighbor, so what? Is that it? Are neighbors no more important than goddamned trees? Do you plant a new one every time one is cut down?"

"There is no other way."

"Yes, Kevin, there is." Millie spoke quietly, but her voice was razor sharp.

"This is none of your affair, Millie. Hush up."

"None of my affair, is it. And I suppose it's your legs they'll be pullin' apart when they decide to pay us a visit. You won't mind it, either, will you. You think Rachel Higgins shouldn't have minded. Is that what you're trying to tell us?"

"Don't be talkin' about such things in front of a stranger. It's not proper. And I'm not talkin' to you, anyway. I'm talking to Cotton."

"But *I* hear you, Kevin. I hear what you're saying and I can't believe my ears. We always knew it would come to this. We used to talk about it, but you didn't want to face it. So we stopped talking about it. We pretended it didn't happen. And when it did happen, we pretended it didn't affect us. It was someone we didn't like. It was someone who was too weak to survive out here. We had a thousand reasons. And now we have a thousand corpses and not one of them deserved to die."

She stood up and walked toward the window. Sweeping the curtain aside, she pointed to the fields beyond the barn. "That's our land, Kevin. Yours and mine. Do you understand that? *Ours!* And we act like it isn't. We act like we don't give a damn."

"What can we do?"

"I'll tell you what we can't do. We can't bring a child into this kind of world. That's one thing we can't do. And I *won't* do it, either."

"Who said anything about a child."

"Nobody. Yet."

He looked at her in confusion. The light seemed to break over him in slow motion. "You're not tellin' me . . ."

"I'm not tellin' you anything, Kevin O'Hara. I'm just saying that I will not bring a child into this world as long as we are here and Ralph Conlee is allowed to roam around like he owns the place. I won't and that's all there is to it."

"Look," Ted cut in, "let's not get away from the main problem, here."

"And what is that?" O'Hara snapped. "Why don't you explain to us, since you seem to have caused it all in the first place."

"Mr. Cotton caused nothing, Kevin. *You* caused it. You and all the other men who stood by and let it happen, instead of doing something about it."

"Alright, alright. Let the man speak. Go ahead, Cotton."

Ted took a deep breath. "We can't change what happened. I'm not saying we can. But I know that a man like Ralph Conlee will want revenge. It's as natural to him as breathing. I'm sorry for that, but it was the right thing to do. It was the *only* thing to do."

"So you tell us."

Ted ignored the sarcasm. "Look, what's important is not what already happened. It's what's going to happen you have to worry about."

"It's out of our hands. You've let the tiger out of his cage."

"No. There never was a cage. That's what you don't seem to understand. The only thing keeping Conlee away from you was chance. Nothing more than that. And until you understand that, there is nothing you can do. As long as you keep lying to yourself, telling yourself that he'll leave you alone as long as you don't provoke him, you won't be able to act. But you're wrong. One day he'll come riding up the lane out there, and that'll be that. It'll be good-bye Kevin and good-bye Millie. The house and barn will be gone to ashes and you two along with them. Is that what you want? Do you want to just sit here and wait for that to happen, or do you want to try and do something about it?"

"What, dammit? What can we do?"

"For one thing, you can get all the farmers together, talk things over. You can set up patrols, you can force the sheriff to use his badge instead of just wearing it."

"And how do we do that?"

"By demanding it. By showing him how, if he's not man enough to do it himself. Stand up for yourselves. You came after Johnny and the boys with hayforks, for chrissakes. They had guns, and you went out, half of you, with garden tools. And you know why you did that?"

"To protect our livestock . . . of course."

"No, dammit, that's not why. You did it because you weren't already beaten. You didn't go out there believing you'd lost. But when it comes to Conlee, there's no contest. He doesn't win. You lose. You lose because you don't have the will not to. He doesn't have to do anything. You hand him the prize and you walk away. No contest."

"Maybe so, but what difference does it make?"

"All the difference in the world. Put yourself in his shoes. Why would you move on, if you knew there was no reason. Other farmers are out there, hundreds, thousands. Conlee doesn't bother them. And the reason he doesn't is because he doesn't have to. Why should he risk his neck to take something from one of them, when you all sit on your hands and give it to him right here, without a fight? He's not a fool."

"Neither am I, Cotton."

"Then stop acting like one, for God's sake."

"Listen to Mr. Cotton, Kevin," Millie said. "He's right, and it's our only chance."

"I don't know . . ." O'Hara shook his head.

"At least we can try, Kevin. We can do that much, can't we?"

For the next three days, they tried. Kevin O'Hara made the rounds. And, one by one, the farmers turned him away. Millie talked to the wives, trying to get them to make their husbands see the light, but three days of rejection convinced her it was pointless. It was too late. They had waited too long, and now no one wanted to risk anything, even if it meant saving his own neck.

On the evening of the third day, Ted sat beside the wagon, talking to Cookie. The old man tried to console him, but it wasn't working.

"You did your best, Teddy. You can't help it if they don't want to listen."

"But they have to listen."

"No, they don't. They don't have to do a damn thing they don't want to. And you can't make 'em, neither."

"But . . ."

"Look, Teddy. Maybe you and me ought to head back to Texas. I'll bet old Rafe is gettin' mighty lonely."

"I can't, Cookie. Not yet."

"Son, you ain't gonna get them sodbusters to do nothin'. And you can't take Conlee on alone. You know that, don't you?"

Ted didn't answer him. Instead, he got up. He was about to walk away when Millie stepped out onto the porch. She carried a lantern turned down low and walked toward the wagon.

"Evenin', ma'am," Ted said.

"Good evening, Mr. Cotton."

"Pretty night, isn't it?"

"No, it isn't. Nothing about this place is beautiful. Not anymore."

"Can't blame it on the world, Mrs. O'Hara. It's people make it this way. What's right is right, and what's pretty is pretty. And it's a pretty night."

Millie shook her head. "You're right. It *is* a pretty night."

"You shouldn't be so hard on Kevin."

"Hard on him?"

"I know how he feels. I was that way, once. After the war, I just . . . I'd had a bellyful of killin'. I . . ."

"You blame yourself for what happened to your brother, don't you?"

"Yes, ma'am, I do."

"It wasn't your fault, you know. You weren't even here."

"Shoulda been."

"That wouldn't have changed things. You might both be dead now. Would that be better?"

"Yes, ma'am, it would."

He walked to his horse. After swinging up into the saddle, he leaned down and patted Millie's shoulder. "We do what we can, Mrs. O'Hara. Seems like, right now, I got to do somethin' I shoulda done before this."

"Where are you going?"

"Same place I go every night."

"I see, and where is that?"

"Never mind."

He kicked the pony and moved off in the darkness. She called after him, but he didn't respond. Still staring into the night, she said, "Where's he going, Cookie?"

"Conlee's camp."

"He can't do that, they'll kill him."

"Oh, he ain't going *in* the camp. Just to watch. One of these nights, Conlee's bound to make a mistake."

"But still . . ."

"He don't want to die, Mrs. O'Hara, if that's what you're thinkin'. But he sure enough wants to kill Ralph Conlee. And he will, too, unless I miss my guess."

"How can you be so sure?"

"Knowed him a long time. He was confused for a while, but he's alright now. Just like his daddy. And his daddy's daddy, I suppose. See, he's a Cotton, and he knows what that means."

"What does it mean, Cookie?"

"Don't know ma'am. I ain't a Cotton."

23

Ted gave up after another fruitless night of watching. Once, he thought he might have hit pay dirt, when a small knot of horsemen left the camp in a hurry. He followed them for five miles before he got a good enough look to know that Conlee wasn't one of them. He thought about following them anyway, taking them on and cutting the odds a little, but if he got killed, it would be a waste.

He didn't mind dying as long as Conlee died first. Anything else was a bad bargain. So he returned to his post and spent half the night, convinced that his day would come. When it was clear Conlee wasn't going anywhere, he mounted up and headed back to the O'Hara farm. Every night the ride got longer. This night was the longest so far, and it seemed like nothing would ever change. The rising sun reminded him of that permanence.

Ted's heart sank when he saw the smoke rising beyond the hill. There was only one farm he knew of in that direction, and the smoke was too voluminous to be the stove or the chimney. Pushing his pony up the next hill, he never broke stride as he crested the ridge and plunged down the far side.

From the next hill, he could see for sure, but there was no doubt in his mind what he'd see. He lashed at the pony, appalled at his own fury, and the pony tried to outrun the sting of the reins, its feet barely touching long enough to complete a stride and start the next.

Careening up the hill, the pony missed a step and stumbled. Ted hung on, but it was too late. The pony fell and Ted flew from the saddle, tumbling forward over its head and landing heavily on his back. Only the thick cushion of grass saved him from serious injury, but it did nothing for the pony. The animal squealed in pain as it tried to rise. Favoring its right front leg, it kept losing its balance and falling back to the ground.

Ted knew, without having to look, that its leg was broken. The animal lay on its side, pawing at the earth with its one good front leg, and Ted climbed to his feet, wiping the dead grass from his clothes. His left shoulder hurt, but nothing seemed to be broken. He walked slowly toward the injured horse and knelt by the quivering head. The pony looked at him, its flat, expressionless eyes following his every movement.

Ted didn't know what to do. He couldn't leave the horse to die, and he couldn't risk a gunshot. He still didn't know what was happening in the next valley, but if it came anywhere close to what he feared, a gunshot now might be his own death knell. He patted the animal on the shoulder and rubbed its muzzle. The horse nickered, bucking its head against his palm. He scratched between its ears, trying to decide what to do.

He didn't really have any choice, but he couldn't bring himself to do it. Not yet. He left the animal behind and started up the slope. He wanted to know for sure what lay ahead of him. Then, if he was convinced that he had no alternative, he'd come back and do what he had to do.

The smoke grew thicker as he climbed, and Ted steeled himself for what he knew was coming. Just below the line of the hill, he dropped to his knees and crept forward like some bizarre medieval penitent. His mouth was dry, and his shoulder was beginning to throb. It wasn't possible to put any weight on his left arm, and every twist of his upper body seared him with a wave of fire.

Then he could see over the hill, and the pain washed away. What he saw was even worse. The chuck wagon, parked a few yards from O'Hara's corral, was a mass of flames. Half a dozen strange horses milled around alongside the corral, some hitched and some dragging their reins. The yard was empty. He saw not a soul.

Ted slammed his fist into the unyielding earth, and the tremor ripped up through his arm and exploded in his left shoulder. He cursed once, so softly he wasn't even sure he'd done it, then crept back away from the hilltop and got to his feet. He sprinted downhill, heedless of the uneven terrain, even half hoping he would break his own leg and someone would put him out of his misery.

He got his saddlebags off the injured pony, pulled the Winchester from the boot, and unsheathed a thick-bladed knife. It was an ugly thing, one he chose not to use, but never failed to carry with him. He'd seen it used during the war. It was the kind popularized and, according to some, invented by the legendary Jim Bowie, and it had a dozen purposes, but only one that really counted. It was meant to kill, quickly and surely.

He knelt again by the horse, patted its neck and allowed the head to rest against his knee. Closing his eyes, he brought the knife against the horse's neck. He felt with blind fingers for the throbbing artery, found it, and pressed the edge of the knife against the pulsing flesh.

He counted to ten, slowing with every number, conscious that time was wasting and yet no more able to speed himself through the ritual than if nothing had been wrong. He tightened his grip on the knife and gritted his teeth.

But he couldn't do it. He cursed again, again softly. Then, resheathing the knife, he draped the saddlebags over his shoulder and turned toward the hill behind him. The first step was the hardest. He trudged upward, away from his own failure, wondering whether it was humanity or cowardice. Even as he neared the crest of the hill, he thought about turning back. But he knew it was no use.

He broke over the ridge, no longer caring whether anyone saw him or not. As he started down the far side, a single gunshot cracked somewhere beyond the house. He saw Kevin O'Hara in the doorway to the barn. It looked for all the world like he was drunk. The big Irishman stumbled once, but kept on staggering toward the house.

A second man appeared in the doorway, a pistol in his hand. Deliberately, he sighted on the Irishman's broad back as Ted dropped to his knee and raised the Winchester. He found the gunman there, a speck just beyond the gunsight, and squeezed slowly. The discharge sounded like thunder, and he saw the gunman fall back into the barn and out of sight. O'Hara fell at the same instant, and Ted got to his feet and started to run. Every step jarred his aching shoulder, but he couldn't stop, even if he wanted to.

Ted recognized Conlee's horse as he drew closer to the house. He cursed himself for a fool and wondered whether Conlee had tricked him, or if it was just coincidence.

He'd seen Kevin, but there was no sign of Millie or Cookie. And Margaret Reynolds was in the house, too. Ted was determined to spare her a repeat of the agony she had already lived through. "If there is a God in heaven," he whispered, "he'll give me the courage and whatever else I need. I don't give a damn what happens to me, but I will not stand for this. Not again."

He ripped open the saddlebags and grabbed a box of shells for the Winchester. He was two hundred yards from the porch when a man stepped out of the front door. The man walked toward the barn and stopped long enough to kick Kevin O'Hara once in passing, the way an angry drunk might kick at a sleeping dog.

The man didn't look back as Ted closed on the house. By the time he reached the door to the barn, Ted was only twenty yards from the house. He sprinted to the right, getting the house between him and the barn. The man was certain to find his dead compatriot on the floor of the barn. Whether he would realize someone other than Kevin O'Hara had shot him was a close call, and Ted couldn't trust the possibility.

Ted left the saddlebags leaning against the house. It sounded quiet inside, and he debated charging in, but he couldn't pass up the chance to narrow the odds a little more. Slipping around the rear of the house, he ducked under a window, tiptoed to the next, and pressed his ear against the window frame. The house was deathly still, and he dropped to his knees to crawl under the second window.

He watched the barn for a moment, just long enough to see whether the raider was visible. When he didn't see him, Ted glanced at the side of the house. There was a single narrow window on that wall, and it was open. He could see the curtains shifting in a slight breeze. It was risky, but he'd have to chance it.

Making a wide loop, Ted sprinted for the side of the barn, running on his toes to muffle his footsteps. He reached the corner of the front wall just as a dull thump sounded inside. A moment later, he heard a horse whinny. He caught the first whiff of smoke as an orange glow suddenly mushroomed deep in the barn. A ball of black smoke rolled out of the door, tumbling over itself in its haste to get out of the barn, then began to disintegrate.

Ted leaned the Winchester against the wall, propping it against the edge of the open door. He crept along the front wall of the barn and pulled the Bowie knife from its sheath. He peered into the barn, expecting the arsonist to dash outside any second.

Flattening his back against the splintery wood, he tiptoed closer. He heard another subdued whoosh, and then hurried footsteps approached the door. Ted steeled himself, ignoring his sweaty grip on the knife. He saw a shadow spill out of the barn, backlit by the orange flame and partially wreathed in acrid black smoke as the hay inside began to burn.

The man stepped through the doorway and Ted sprang, locking his left arm around the man's neck and dragging him back into the barn. The man struggled, and he outweighed Ted by a good twenty pounds. The pain in his shoulder was fierce as Ted struggled to haul the man back and out of sight.

Tightening his grip around the throat, trying to shut down the man's air with his forearm, he brought the knife up and hesitated for just a second. The man mumbled something through his compressed larynx and Ted slashed once, sweeping the blade across the throat just below his arm. He felt a gush of sticky warmth splatter his sleeve. The blood soaked in, and the sleeve quickly stuck to his skin.

A horrible gurgle sounded as the man tried to breathe through his severed windpipe. Ted squeezed a little tighter as the man's struggles grew more feeble. One foot kicked at him twice, then seemed to dangle. Suddenly the stench of voided bowels swirled around him, and Ted was back in Farley's Field. He thought for a moment of how white and still the steeple of Shiloh Church had looked in a burst of sunlight. He remembered thinking then how obscene it was that a church should be forced to bear witness to such slaughter.

He had no such misgivings this time. He welcomed the stench. He relished the sticky warmth soaking his sleeve. It had come to this, and it seemed at last as if he was within sight of an answer to his questions. No matter what happened, they would not torment him again when this was all over. If he died, so be it, and if not, at least he would know that he was capable of doing what had to be done, no matter how merciless that knowledge might be.

The last gurgle died and the body collapsed against him. He shoved the man to one side, not even bothering to watch the body crumble into a heap against the wall.

Ted walked to the door of the barn. He retrieved the Winchester and started across the broad yard. Then, remembering the horses, he changed course and shooed them away, hacking at the reins of those hitched to the corral and flapping his hat to chase them all.

He had just started back toward the front porch when the first scream seemed to tear the house open. The curtains billowed in the solitary window as if the house itself were screaming. Ted wiped the blade of the knife on his thigh as he started to run.

A second scream echoed across the yard, and Ted tossed away the Winchester. He headed straight for the open window, picking up speed as he closed on it. At the side of the house, he slowed and crept to the glass. It was dark inside, and he could barely see. He blinked away the sunlight, waiting for his eyes to adjust.

When they did, he gasped. Millie O'Hara, the bodice torn from her dress, struggled to free herself from the grasp of two men, one of whom pawed at her breasts while the other wound her hair around his fist and dragged her to the floor. Little Margaret lay on the floor, bleeding from an ugly wound on her right temple. And as Ted watched, Ralph Conlee lowered himself and covered the frail body with his own.

24

Ted backed away a few steps and sprinted for the window. Gathering his legs under him like coiling springs, he launched himself through the air and covered his head with his arms. He narrowly missed the window frame, felt it graze his left shoulder, and landed on his stomach. He slid across the rough boards of the floor and skidded to a halt.

He rolled to one side, swinging the Colt around, and fired once, then again. In the closed room, the gunshots sounded like sticks of dynamite. The first bullet caught one of the raiders grappling with Millie. The man clutched at his left shoulder until the second bullet smashed through his collarbone, breaking it with a loud crack. Blood smeared the wall behind him as he slid to the floor.

Millie stared at Ted for a long moment,

as stunned as everyone else in the room, then covered her mouth with her hands. Everything seemed to move so slowly. Ted saw things clearly, sharply, as if the room had suddenly been bathed in brilliant light.

Millie's second captor turned as Ted got to his feet. The man shoved Millie away and she slammed into the wall beside the fireplace. Her head cracked against the rough stone and she slid to the floor. The guerrilla, a man squat as a toad, with bulging blue eyes that looked watery even in the dim light, growled as he reached for his gun.

Ted swung the muzzle of the Colt around and squeezed the trigger again. The hammer fell on a dead round and Ted fanned the hammer back again, squeezed just as the man dove to one side. The Colt jerked in Ted's hand and the bullet just missed. Firing again, he nailed the man as he tried to roll away from the gun and pinned himself against a table leg. He groaned and tried to sit up. Ted took two quick steps, bringing his leg back and snapping it forward. His boot caught the toadlike man under the chin, snapping his head back and into the thick edge of the oaken tabletop.

Ted whirled as Conlee scrambled to his

feet. The guerrilla leader found himself covered by Ted's gun. Conlee backed away, reaching for Margaret, but the girl crabbed away from the clutching fingers. It was suddenly quiet in the room. Conlee wavered a bit, almost like a drunk trying to convince the world he was sober.

"So," he said. The big man's voice was loud in the confined space. "I reckon you think you got me. That right?"

Ted ignored him. He bent at the knees and grabbed a revolver from the floor.

"Because you better know this," Conlee continued, his raspy baritone scraping the silence from the walls and echoing from one high corner of the room. "I don't kill easily, cowboy. Not at all."

Ted still kept silent. Margaret crawled into a corner. She started to whimper, and Ted remembered his promise that she would be safe, that she no longer had to worry about Conlee or anyone like him.

"You're an animal, Conlee, a fucking animal."

"I'm afraid you have the advantage of me, cowboy. You know my name and I don't know yours."

"No need," Ted said.

"Man always needs to know who tries to kill him. It ain't natural, otherwise."

"Did you tell my brother that before you killed him?"

Conlee shrugged. "Depends. Who are you?"

"Ted Cotton. You killed my brother a few weeks back."

"Sorry, don't know no Cottons."

Ted was getting worried. He could almost see the wheels turning in Conlee's head. The man was angling for something, trying to stall, but why?

He did a quick tally, then he knew, and his blood flash froze in his veins, his heart skipped a beat, then another. There had been six strange horses outside. He could only account for five men. Where was the sixth?

And where was Cookie?

Conlee smiled as if he'd been reading Ted's mind. "That's right, cowboy. You ain't home yet, not by a damn sight."

Ted waved the barrel of his own Colt toward the door. "Outside," he said.

Conlee tilted his head, and the grin seemed to slide that way as if it were a mask thrown out of kilter by gravity. He shook his head agreeably. "Whatever you say, Cotton."

"Don't talk," Ted snapped. "Just walk. Double quick."

"Army man, was you? Secesh bastard, to be sure. But I respect that, a man fighting for what he believes in."

"I told you to shut up. You open your mouth for anything but air and I swear to God, I'll kill you. You understand me?"

Conlee nodded, but the grin widened. "Sure thing, cowboy. Whatever you say."

He stepped toward the door, and Ted watched him, moving around the table to keep the big man's hands in plain sight. Where the hell was Cookie?

And where was the sixth man?

"Alright, Conlee, turn around."

Conlee stopped in his tracks. He turned slowly, and Ted snapped, "Hurry up. Get your hands up on your shoulders. And keep 'em there."

Conlee complied slowly. Ted heard a stirring in a corner, but didn't dare take his eyes off the big man. "Now, back through the door. One step at a time. Take it slow. Take two and I'll shoot you."

"You're not the type, Reb. You ain't got the sand to shoot a man like me."

"What sort of man is that?" He knew Conlee was trying to slow things down, to drag it out until something happened, but there was a serpentine fascination to the man. Ted couldn't help himself. And he couldn't bring himself to gun the man down in cold blood, not in front of Millie and the girl. Conlee backed through the door, step by step, just as he was told. He never lost his grin. As he backed into the morning sunlight, he blinked until his eyes adjusted. When he stopped fluttering his lids, the eyes sat in his face glittering like two black marbles. They were devoid of feeling. Snake eyes. They pinned Ted and never left him.

Ted stepped through the doorway and Conlee backed up a step, nearly losing his footing as he stepped off the porch onto the ground. "You should have warned me about that, cowboy. What's wrong with you? I coulda broke my neck." The grin widened, but the eyes never changed.

"Soon enough for that, Conlee."

The big man laughed. "You ain't got a prayer, you know that?"

"Yes," Ted said. "I do know that. But you don't either, so I guess we're evenly matched."

"Not exactly," Conlee said. "Not exactly."

"I know what you're thinking, but it doesn't make any difference. I know there's another savage here somewhere, but it won't help you none, Conlee. None at all."

Conlee laughed again. It was surprisingly rich laughter, welling up from somewhere deep in his gut and echoing through the barrel chest as it rushed out of him like a spring flood.

Ted smiled, in spite of himself. "Over there," he said, waving the captured revolver toward the ruins of the mess wagon.

Conlee turned to see where Ted was pointing. "Oh, forget about that, my friend. The old man ain't gonna help you, neither."

"Move." The single word cracked like a bullwhip, and Conlee seemed startled for the first time, as if he was beginning to lose his confidence. He started to turn, but Ted stopped him. "Backward . . ."

Conlee nodded. "You're the man with the gun, hoss."

They were halfway across the yard when he heard the scream. Ted jerked his head around for a split second and Conlee started to move, but Ted pulled the hammer back and waved the pistol.

"Stay right there!"

"Tide's changin', hoss."

"We'll see."

Glancing toward the door, Ted saw Millie in the shadows. She stumbled through the doorway and behind her was the sixth man. He snaked an arm around Millie's neck and held a revolver up where Ted could see it for a moment. Then he pressed the muzzle against Millie's head.

"Looks like time's up, cowboy," Conlee said.

The man on the porch shouted, "Drop the gun."

"You won't shoot her," Ted said. His voice trembled, but he tried to tough it out. "Or I'll shoot Conlee."

"You think I give a damn, cowboy? Try me."

He cocked the pistol and forced Millie off the step. She was naked from the waist up, and it was that violation, more than the gun, that enraged Ted. "Let her go, damn you."

"Can't do that. I'll kill her. I mean it, now."

"You'll kill her anyway," Ted said.

"Now that's just the chance you have to take, hoss," Conlee said.

Ted moved to the side a bit, trying to keep both men in sight. Conlee took a step and Ted shook his head. "Don't . . ."

Conlee waved a hand. "No hurry. I got all day, cowboy."

It crossed Ted's mind that he should shoot Conlee first, but he knew the man on the porch would kill Millie. He was beaten, but he couldn't accept it. Not yet.

Conlee took another step, and Ted shouted, "Back up, God damn you. Back up! Now!"

Conlee stood his ground. Millie started to cry, and the man on the porch tightened his grip around her neck. "Shut up, damn you." Millie continued to sob, but she tried to swallow the sound.

"Make you a deal, hoss," Conlee said.

"No deals."

"Now, don't make up your mind until you hear it. How about you take the woman and the girl? You take our guns, and you ride out of here. That way, nobody gets hurt. How's that sound?"

"No deals."

"Now that don't sound much like a man's got balls." He laughed, then shouted to the man on the porch. "How about it, Jace, sound like a man with balls to you?" He took another step forward. Ted saw it, but didn't know how to stop it.

Conlee took another step.

The gunshot surprised them all for a moment. Then Conlee charged. Ted fired his Colt. The bullet caught Conlee in the chest. He grunted and staggered a step, then regained his momentum. The big man charged ahead and Ted squeezed the trigger of the other gun. The hammer fell on an empty chamber. Ted thumbed it back and squeezed again as Conlee barreled into him. The impact knocked both men to the ground.

Ted cracked the pistol against Conlee's skull, but it just enraged the big man. He locked his hands around Ted's throat and Ted rapped him again and again with the empty pistol.

Conlee hung on like a lamprey, locking his arms and putting all his weight into the stranglehold. Ted was starting to choke. He remembered the knife and jerked it loose. Conlee saw it and started to let go as Ted slammed the blade into his side. The big man groaned as Ted sliced across his gut. Both hands locked on Ted's wrist, but the strength was gone. Ted tried to get up, putting all his weight into the effort and forcing Conlee back with the knife itself.

The big man fell backward and Ted kicked free. He scrambled to his feet and looked toward the porch. Millie, her hands over her mouth, was motionless. She seemed frozen in midscream. The sound poured from her in one continuous howl.

The dead man sprawled half on the

porch and half off. Behind him, framed in the doorway, Margaret stood crying, the pistol still smoking in her hand.

25

Ted shoveled the last of the dirt onto the mound. He tamped it down with the flat of the blade. Grabbing the makeshift sign, hacked out of charred siding and bearing only the single word "Cookie," he stabbed it into the damp earth and drove it home with a blow of the shovel. Millie and Margaret bent to place a few flowers.

"He was a good friend to you, wasn't he?" Millie asked.

Ted nodded. "Yeah, he was a good friend."

"I'm sorry."

Ted didn't answer.

"What are you going to do now?" Millie asked.

"Dunno." He thought about Texas. Somebody had to tell Rafe about Cookie. But the thought of facing Jacob and Ellie frightened him. He didn't think he could do it. And he didn't think he wanted to. Still, he had to tell Rafe. "Texas, I guess. How about you?"

"I don't know. I have nothing here. And with Kevin . . ." She choked back a sob, and he saw her wipe at a tear. "I guess . . ."

"Look, you can come to Texas, if you want."

"I couldn't. I . . ."

"Why not?"

Millie walked away a few steps. Her back to him, she stared at the ashes of the barn and the house. "We could take Margaret, too," Ted said. "I mean . . . you know, until we can get word to her family."

Millie turned back to him. "I don't think so," she said.

"No, I suppose not." He threw the shovel aside. He sighed, realizing he'd never visited Johnny's grave and didn't know where it was.

"You going to stay here, then?" he asked.

"I guess I will."

Ted walked to his horse and climbed into the saddle. "I might be back," he said. "I got some things to take care of first, but I'll be back."

Millie walked close to the horse. She reached out for his hand. He remembered the strong grip. He smiled, just for a second. Then he took her hand.

"See you," he said.

"Yes."

At the end of the lane, he turned in the saddle. Millie was still watching. Margaret waved, then started to run. Millie was right behind her.

The employees of Thorndike Press hope you have enjoyed this Large Print book. All our Thorndike and Wheeler Large Print titles are designed for easy reading, and all our books are made to last. Other Thorndike Press Large Print books are available at your library, through selected bookstores, or directly from us.

For information about titles, please call:

(800) 223-1244

or visit our Web site at:

www.gale.com/thorndike
www.gale.com/wheeler

To share your comments, please write:

Publisher
Thorndike Press
295 Kennedy Memorial Drive
Waterville, ME 04901